For the Hope of a Crow

(Red Dead Mayhem, Book 1)

T. S. JOYCE

For the Hope of a Crow

ISBN-13: 978-1981719416573
ISBN-10: 1719416575
Copyright © 2018, T. S. Joyce
First electronic publication: May 2018

T. S. Joyce
www. tsjoyce.com

NOTE FROM THE AUTHOR:

Published in the United States of America

First digital publication: May 2018
First print publication: May 2018

Editing: Corinne DeMaagd
Cover Photography: Wander Aguiar
Cover Model: Tyler Halligan

DEDICATION

For Lo.
Thanks for asking for this shifter.
This one is for you.

ACKNOWLEDGMENTS

I couldn't write these books without some amazing people behind me. A huge thanks to Corinne DeMaagd, for helping me to polish my books, and for being an amazing and supportive friend. Looking back on our journey here, it makes me smile so big. You are an incredible teammate, C!

Thanks to Tyler Halligan, the cover model for this book and several others. Any time I get the chance to work with him, I take it because he is so fun to work with. TnT! Thank you to Wander Aguiar and his amazing team for this shot for the cover. You always get the perfect image for what I'm needing.

And last but never least, thank you, awesome reader. You have done more for me and my stories than I can even explain on this teeny page. You found my books, and ran with them, and every share, review, and comment makes release days so incredibly special to me.

1010 is magic and so are you.

ONE

Click.

The sound of a gun being cocked jolted Ramsey Hunt from deep sleep.

On instinct, he reached for the Glock he kept on the nightstand, but when he stretched out his fingertips, they weren't fingers at all, but feathers. And the gun he'd heard was staring him straight in the face. The only thing that moved was his pounding heart.

He wasn't in bed at all, but in the woods. No...he was in Two Claws Woods, and the man holding the handgun to his face was none other than the Alpha of the New Darby Clan, Kurt. Behind him, Ten stood shivering in her human skin, an oversize T-shirt

3

wrapped tight around her. It wasn't that cold, though.

"You said you would leave me alone," she murmured, her shaking voice matching her body. Shit. She sounded scared.

"Caw!" Fuck, he couldn't explain in this form, but a Change would mean standing naked in front of a loaded weapon while hoping Kurt didn't pull that trigger and paint the mud with his brain matter. Already, the dark-haired man was snarling a feral sound, and his eyes were glowing light silver.

Ramsey backed away, wings tucked tightly to his side so he looked smaller, never taking his eyes off the barrel of that weapon. The grass underfoot tickled, and the breeze was warm where it lifted his feathers the wrong way. Summer had come to Montana, but his blood stayed chilled all the time.

Kurt lowered the weapon, and for an instant, Ramsey felt relief. Mercy. Kurt was granting him mercy. Or so he thought until the jackass pulled the trigger and blasted a shot at the ground by Ramsey's talons. Pain sliced against his hip, burning red hot. Fuckin' mountain lion. He'd shot too close. Didn't he know anything about ricochet? From the feral smile on Kurt's face, he didn't care.

Ramsey beat his wings against the hot wind and lifted into the air. And just as he turned to leave these awful woods, he caught a glimpse of Tenlee's face. She looked like she was about to cry. She looked sad that he was even here. While Ramsey...Ramsey...he was only sad she couldn't see him like he saw her—worthy.

He left them behind and flew up, up until it was only him and the stars and the moon, and the rest of the world was far below. Warmth trickled from where the bullet had grazed his underbelly, but he couldn't bring himself to overly care. If he died, he died. There were worse ways to go than bleeding out mid-air and falling to the earth.

He was going crazy.

Ramsey flew faster, over the night lights of the small town of Darby. He was going crazy because his mate had chosen another, and his crow would never be able to cope with the loss. This is what happened to shifters like him. To shifters who mated for life. To shifters who bonded to someone who didn't bond to them back. They got worse and worse and worse until they couldn't even see straight, and then they made mistakes that got them killed.

5

Only Ramsey wasn't the only one at risk. He was Alpha of Red Dead Mayhem. He had an entire murder of crows bonded to him, propping him up, and when he fell, he would take them with him.

They would all go crazy because of him.

Because he hadn't been able to keep the mate his crow had chosen.

A broken mating bond started out as sleepwalking. He had been waking up all over the small town of Corvallis. And then it had progressed to Darby, a ten-minute flight away. Now, apparently, his crow was suicidal because he was fine sitting in front of a damn pistol in the hand of a mountain lion shifter. Volatile creatures, those.

The lights of Corvallis appeared below him, so he dipped down, gliding easily on the warm wind currents. He could make out the clubhouse for his MC, Red Dead Mayhem. They'd weeded out the surrounding businesses one shop owner at a time. Crows were territorial. They'd bullied and pestered until the small businesses directly around them had folded. A dick-move, sure, but secretly, he'd been sending business to their new shops and throwing money at them, too. It wasn't like he didn't respect small business. Crows just didn't like humans too close, and especially not near a clubhouse. The deeds of crows weren't always for the good of society.

The large wooden sign for the clubhouse didn't state the MC's name. Instead, it just had a red painting of a crow with paint dripping down. Ethan Blackwood, his Second, had made it when they'd first bought the place. If he had he been born human, he could've had a promising career selling his paintings in studios. But he was born a crow, with a monstrous bloodline, and crows had rebel blood, so mostly he just did graffiti art around the cities they visited. The art always depicted crows. Ethan was more territorial than most. He was also having the hardest time with Ramsey's order not to murder the entire Two Claws Clan and force Tenlee back here.

Ramsey needed to keep his shit together. Ethan would come for his Alpha rank soon. And the Clan would back Ethan because everyone knew what was coming for Ramsey—insanity.

He dipped toward the parking lot behind the club and spread his wings, angling his body to slow himself. And right before he landed on the ground, he Changed, just like he'd done a thousand times before.

A few of the MC were sitting on an old bench near the row of motorcycles out front, but they stopped talking when they saw Ramsey. God, he hated this. The Clan had gone to hell since the war with Two Claws. "The fuck are you looking at?" he barked at Trey, the most dominant of the three.

"Nothing, Alpha," Trey murmured, but his eyes were the pitch black of his crow, and there was a smirk on his lips.

Asshole was cruising for an ass-whoopin. It had been two days since a good fight, and Crazy Ramsey was due.

But first, he needed something to dull the pain in his head, his body...and his heart. Fuck. Tenlee had messed everything up. She had no idea what she'd done, what destruction she had caused.

She had doomed Ramsey.

Rike was behind the bar. Thank God, because Ramsey couldn't deal with Ethan's shit tonight.

The dark-haired, tatted-up giant dragged his attention from a couple of Crow Chasers to Ramsey. "'Scuse me, ladies, I'll be right back." He twitched his chin toward the end of the bar. "A word?" he asked Ramsey.

"Not tonight, Rike. Give me the good stuff."

Rike looked down at Ramsey's hand that was shaking. Ramsey followed his gaze and clenched his fist to cover it up. "We got a fuckin' problem? Whiskey. That's the only words you get tonight."

"Where were you?"

"Where I wanted to be," Ramsey lied in a growl. He sidled the counter and yanked an unopened bottle of Jameson from the cabinet, then strode toward the stairs. "Meeting in the morning."

"You actually gonna show up to this one?"

"What did you say?" Ramsey yelled, rounding on his Third.

Rike looked around as everyone dipped to silence. Swallowing hard, Rike tucked his chin to his chest and angled his head. Even crows knew submission. He cleared his throat then said, "You called a meeting tonight."

Ramsey felt like someone had socked him in the face with iron knuckles. "What?"

"You called a meeting. It's why everyone is at the clubhouse. We waited a couple hours, but you never showed."

Ramsey parted his lips to call him a

motherfuckin' liar, but it sounded familiar. Had he? Had he called a meeting? And then sleepwalked through it?

Ramsey clenched his shaking hands harder. "Meeting is rescheduled for tomorrow morning. Something came up tonight."

There was pity in Rike's eyes. *Pity.* Of all the emotions a crow could show, Ramsey hated pity the most. He ripped his attention from the Third, scanned the mess of people crowded around the bar and pool tables, then turned his back on all of them, made his way to the stairs, and got out of their line of sight as fast as possible.

He was still king here, but his crown was slipping.

He took the stairs two at a time until he reached the hallway up top. There were four doors, two on each side—three bedrooms for when the boys were too drunk to ride home and a bathroom. There was also a hidden room that was stacked with money and guns, but that didn't have a door in the hallway. That one had floor access from the room he walked into at the end.

He didn't have a home outside of the club. This was it. His room. His life. Or the end of it, at least.

Ramsey popped the top on the bottle and tipped it back, drank until his throat was on fire. He sat down in the chair in the darkest corner of the room. His body just...ached. Chronic pain was enough to send a person over the edge without a broken mating bond. Nothing felt right, and this headache was a year old. It had started when his mate ran away. Ramsey shook his head, trying to dislodge the confusion. "Not my mate," he growled. "Kurt's mate."

Christ, his head hurt. He chugged another eight gulps and slammed the bottle onto the end table. Whiskey spewed out the neck, and he damn near cracked the glass, but he didn't have a single ounce of give-a-damn in him right now.

His body was humming to Change again. Great. He couldn't even pass out into unconsciousness to get away from this hell he was living, or he would sleep-fly right back to her.

She was going to have Kurt's babies.

Ramsey buried his face in his hands. He'd made mistakes. He'd treated her like an object, but it was better than he'd been raised! His father had been a monster to his mom, and Ramsey had tried so hard to be better than him. He'd watched Tenlee in her first

Changes out in the woods near Corvallis, struggling with her new, human side. She was an Origin and hadn't started Changing into a human until she was an adult. He'd watched her out in those woods, scared, alone, crying...and his crow had decided in those hours that she was his to protect. His to save.

Only Tenlee had never needed saving, and so now what did he do? What purpose did his crow have? Ramsey the man ran the biggest Clan of crows in existence and was fulfilled. Ramsey the crow was on a downward spiral that had started with every disgusted look Tenlee had given him when he'd tried to touch her.

His middle felt like it was caving in. With a grunt, he ran his hands through his hair and gripped his neck as hard as he could, just to keep his head from splitting apart.

Creeeeak.

Ramsey jerked his attention to the door. It opened slowly, and in slipped Sabrina. She was a Crow Chaser, as he and the boys called the girls who hung around the club. They all looked the same to Ramsey. Hair color didn't matter. They all wore dark shimmery make-up around their eyes and bold red lipstick. Leather jackets, black ripped-up jeans, and sky-high heels that looked uncomfortable as fuck. Sabrina smelled like cigarette smoke and hairspray and desperation.

"Rike sent me up for you," she purred, peeling her leather jacket back from her shoulders. She looked at him directly, daring him to enjoy her slow tease. Sabrina let the jacket slip to the floor and slowly unfastened her jeans. "He says you need something to take your mind off everything, and I got just what you need."

"An easy pussy?" he deadpanned. "That's what Rike thinks I need?"

She'd probably practiced that pout in the mirror a dozen times, but it wasn't going to work on him.

"If I wanted tail, I could get it myself," he gritted out.

"Yeah, well, you gotta rep to maintain, and you ain't had tail in a while. Everyone has been paying attention, Ramsey." Her eyes flashed with fire, and she peeled her shirt over her head. Well, there were her tits, and yeah, she looked hot. Really hot.

Ramsey sighed and sank back in the chair, considering what she'd said. "The boys are keeping up with my sex life?"

"Yep. Can't you feel it, Ramsey? All eyes are on you. Everyone notices every little thing you do different. You ain't fucking the girls no more."

"Because I have a mate."

"Had. *Had* a mate, and was she ever really yours? She didn't even want to be around you. Alpha of Red Dead Mayhem, you had a line of girls ready to do anything you wanted, even that kinky shit, but where were your eyes at? Tenlee, that frigid bitch— *Gasp!*"

Ramsey's hand was around her throat before he even knew he had moved from the chair. "Watch your words about Ten."

Sabrina's eyes flashed with pleasure. This one liked it rough. "Why?" she gasped out, leaning into his grip with a red-painted smile. "She ain't one of us. Never was."

Ramsey snarled but then looked down at her breasts, angry yet strangely turned on. At least there was that. At least his dick was working. He gentled his grip on her throat and pulled her toward him until their cheeks rested against each other. In her ear, he murmured, "You want this? You want an emotionless fuck? No strings? You want me to pound you until you lose yourself?"

"Yes," she whispered, her voice shaky with need.

Too easy. Too easy, and his heart was still all fucked up over Tenlee. As much as he wished he could do the same thing—get lost—he couldn't make himself fuck her. She was too easy, and he would wake up even sicker in the head. He didn't need a helping of guilt piled on top of the mountain of shit he already had to deal with.

Before Tenlee, he would've been inside Sabrina already. He could stay detached and have two girls a night. His appetite had grown insatiable, and he'd kept the Chasers happy. And they kept him steady.

Love.

Love ruined everything.

Love had ruined him.

Ruined something as simple as sex.

Ramsey backed away from her so fast Sabrina stumbled forward and caught herself on the edge of the bed.

"Asshole," she said, grabbing her shirt and jacket from the floor.

"Never pretended to be anything else."

Sabrina gave him one last fiery glare before she

slipped through the door and slammed it closed behind her.

Tomorrow, Ramsey was going to beat Rike's ass. He wouldn't feel any guilt about that.

Bloodlust was the only thing that made him feel better anymore.

TWO

The crow on the sign was downright disturbing. Why had someone painted it in red? And there were grungy drips and splatters that made it look like the crow was bleeding out.

It was raining, but Vina couldn't make herself take another step toward the crow's clubhouse.

This was the address Sarah, the matchmaker, had given her. How had she lived in Darby this long and not known about this Red Dead Mayhem clubhouse? It was only a twenty-five-minute drive from her duplex. She'd taken an interest in the crows a few years ago and asked around about them, but the clubhouse had never come up in casual conversation.

Would Sarah really send her to someplace this

scary? Her trust in the matchmaker wavered.

But okay, he was the first crow to apply for the shifter matchmaking program, and Vina had been waiting for this. Didn't matter who he was…only that he would be hers. And yeah, she got how messed up that was, but she'd accepted her faults long ago. And the one in the lead today was choosing a man as a mate she hadn't even met.

Desperate times and measures and all.

There was a row of motorcycles out front along with several big, beefy, tattooed, bearded men. Most of them were talking low and staring at her, but she was used to that. Vina had an innate ability to stick out like a sore thumb everywhere she went. A lot of that had to do with her inability to dress appropriately for each occasion, and part of it was how she looked—all lanky legged and tall, wild sandy-colored hair, eyes so dark brown they were almost black, and skin the color of a happy summer cloud. She was no classic beauty and, to top that off, she was clumsy as hell. What a terrible shifter she made.

Her new white canvas low-top shoes already had mud splatters on them from her short walk from her car to the middle of the parking lot. Her bare legs were covered in goosebumps from the chilly breeze, her shorts were too short by most people's standards, and her white T-shirt was a direct misstep on such a rainy day. Her petal-pink bra was definitely showing. Mother trucker. She'd brushed her hair today just for this meeting, but all the moisture in the air had made it go wild again, and in her arms was clutched one organized binder with everything Sarah had sent her about Ramsey.

She'd wanted to ask in town about the Alpha of Red Dead Mayhem but had changed her mind because she wanted to figure him out for herself and form her own unbiased opinion about her new mate. Plus, the only thing she needed to know was already checked off—he was a crow, and crows were loyal. Ramsey would be good enough.

"Are you lost?" one of the bikers yelled none-too-politely from under an awning near a garage.

"No," she called, blinking hard as raindrops pelted her face. "I'm just...gathering my courage."

"For what? This ain't no public bar. Piss off."

Horrid, horrid manners. She should Change and stomp him into oblivion. Feeling quite offended, Vina marched toward the door, threw it open with relish, and then froze in the entryway to the Red Dead Mayhem clubhouse. There was a bar across the room where three men sat staring at her over their shoulders. One dark-haired bartender with tattoos all over his neck and arms had his mouth hanging open. One couple, who must have been truly in love, were going at it like rabbits against a pool table, while a couple other men watched casually as though this behavior happened all the time.

Monsters.

Maybe she'd been wrong about the crows.

No, no, no, give them a chance. They are loyal, and that's why you're here.

Well, no matter what, Ramsey wasn't going to be banging her against a pool table. They would have sex. Normal sex. Missionary style with the lights dimmed, and she would possibly give him a BJ on his birthdays and major holidays. She'd written a list of rules for this pairing, and that one was number three. The sex would be...normal. Because normal equaled healthy.

What if he wasn't her type?

"You came?" said the man behind the bar.

"That's what she said," gritted out the man slamming into the girl on the pool table. She was moaning now.

Geez, this was so weird and awful! "Uh, yes, I'm here," Vina said to the bartender lamely. She studied the man. He was covered in tattoos, weighed twice as much as her in muscle, and had a knife on his belt. The giant looked truly rough around the edges, but his black hair was clean and spiked up like a hotboy, and his eyes were a soft brown and clear. He had straight white teeth, full lips under a perfectly trimmed beard, and though she'd never been attracted to gym rats, he filled his gray Harley Davidson tank top out nicely.

"Are you Ramsey?" she asked, failing to keep the hope from her voice. He was cute.

"You look like a suburban housewife," said one of the fellas who was openly watching the couple in their act of debauchery. He had a huge beard that came down past his nipples. "What are you wearing on your feet?"

Vina scoffed. "They are Converses. They are cool!"

The men laughed, even the one slamming into the groaning woman.

Nipple Beard asked, "What the fuck do you want with Ramsey?"

Okay, Vina was having trouble keeping her eyes off the screwing couple since they were both panting. The man had his jeans down to the middle of his thighs as he pummeled her from behind, his buttcheeks flexing with the effort. Did crows only mate from behind? Aaaand now the guy was yelling out, twitching into the girl, and this was the most uncomfortable, embarrassing moment of her life.

"The show ain't free," Nipple Beard said. "This place is club members only, and you haven't answered my question. What do you want with Ramsey?"

"Oh...uuuuuuh..."

"She's good," the bartender said, sauntering around the bar. "I'm Rike," he said, introducing himself with a firm handshake.

Disappointment swirled in her chest. So this one was not her mate. Ramsey could still be that older, beer-gutted, rude gentleman on the wall.

"This way," Rike said, making his way toward a stairwell. Okay, relief. At least Ramsey wasn't one of the depraved guys down here.

At the end of a long hallway, Rike stopped and gave the last door a soft knock.

"Fuck off," came the muffled answer.

Rike gave her a sympathetic smile and said, "Good luck." Then he turned on his heel and was back to the stairs in the time it took her to blink once. Crows were fast.

"What am I supposed to do?" she called out.

"Talk to your mate!" Rike yelled as he disappeared.

Vina huffed in irritation. She was going to give Sarah a very mediocre review.

She lifted her closed fist, hesitated for the span of two seconds to pump herself up, then knocked out the drum beat for "Smells Like Teen Spirit" by Nirvana. She continued knocking until the door yanked open, and there stood one very angry, very muscular, very tattooed man with sleep-mussed hair and wearing a pair of black sweats. His eyes matched the color, which was equal parts terrifying and intriguing. There was no white in his eyes, only the color of coal.

"What. Do. You. Want?" he snarled.

"Uh..."

"It's a simple question."

"Well, I haven't been asked that before! What do I want?" Then she repeated it in a whisper, really thinking about it. "I guess I want a happy life, a stable one, with someone who will buy me ice cream when I'm on my period, and people to care about my birthday parties, or just me in general, pizza parties on Fridays and more time off work would be nice. Vacations wouldn't be horrible either. I also have this thing where I make origami swans when I'm stressed out, so maybe a gift card to the paper shop in town?"

Ramsey slow blinked and then arched an eyebrow. "Lady, I'm drunk, and you look like a soccer mom. I'm real confused on why you are standing in my clubhouse knocking 'Smells Like Teen Spirit' on my door at fucking six in the morning."

"It's ten."

"What?"

"Ten-ten, actually," she said, frowning at her phone. "I was right on time when I came here."

"Do we have a meeting or something? Are you an insurance sales...person?" He dropped his black eyes to her feet. "You ain't a Crow Chaser, that's for damn sure."

"Seriously? Are you insulting my shoes, too? I bought these especially for today. To meet you. And you're staring at them like they are bugs. And not cute bugs, like caterpillars or ladybugs, but one of those gross bugs with a hundred-million legs." Vina hugged the folder to her chest like a shield. "I'm Vina. Vina Fiona Marsh."

"Lady. I don't care." Ramsey was scrubbing his hand up and down his face as he swayed on his feet. "Did you say it's ten?"

"It's ten-eleven now."

"Shit. It was weird to meet you. Don't get stabbed on your way out." Ramsey turned slowly, gripping the doorframe as if he was struggling to keep his balance, and then stepped gingerly toward a bathroom on the other side of the room.

"Um, we were supposed to meet at ten. Sarah set this up?"

"Don't know a Sarah."

Wait, what? Vina hovered on the other side of the open doorway, so uncertain about everything. About every single step that had gotten her here. This didn't feel right, but she had to make sure before she left. Had to figure out what was going on.

"You're Ramsey Hunt, right?" she called, stepping through the doorway and over a guitar on the floor. The room was a wreck. It looked like someone had broken in and destroyed the place looking for something. "Were you robbed?"

"No." He hadn't bothered shutting the bathroom door, so she could clearly see him splashing water on his face.

Okay, so Ramsey Hunt was just a slob then. There were two empty bottles of whiskey on a small end table by a chair in the corner. The sheets on the bed were disheveled, and the floor was covered with papers and clothes. There was a backpack and a baseball bat that had seen some serious damage. A laptop sat open on the floor next to a broken lamp, and almost every pillow from the bed was scattered around the room. One was ripped up...or...no. Vina squinted her eyes at the handle sticking out of it. Oh good, he'd stabbed his pillow.

"I think there has been some sort of mistake," she murmured, her heart sinking to her toes.

"Lady—"

"Vina. Please."

Ramsey sighed an irritated sound and locked his

arms against the sink, stared at her through the mirror, water dripping from his jaw. "Vina. My whole life is a mistake. You're going to have to be really fuckin' specific today. What do you want from me?"

"I think my answer is nothing."

Ramsey frowned in the mirror and then turned around, leaned his butt against the sink, and crossed his arms over his defined chest. Lookey at all those tattoos and flexed-up muscle. His hair was gold-blond, shaved on the sides and longer up top, and his eyes had lightened from pure black to bright blue. He might be a stabby psychopath, but he was a hot stabby psychopath. He canted his head and dragged his focus up and down her body. And ooooh, she didn't know how he did it, but she felt as if he had touched her with his gaze. She took two steps back, and her breath sped up.

"Then what are you doing here?"

"I..." Vina cleared her throat and dropped her eyes to the floor. "I'm your mate."

There were thirty seconds of complete silence. It had stretched on for so long she finally found the courage to look back up at him.

The second they locked eyes, he said, "Have all

the women in this world lost their goddamn minds?"

"I haven't lost my mind! I came here to meet you, as set up by Sarah, our matchmaker!"

"Are you trying to get fucked, too?" Ramsey asked. "Seriously? This is the game?"

"Get fucked, too? That doesn't sound like a game at all. That sounds horrible. I would only *make love*, not *get fucked*. I've read articles on how, if you call it fucking, it negates any intimacy you could have. You could kill the healthy parts of our relationship with destructive words like that."

"Of our relationship?" he barked. His eyes were so wide, and he was looking at her like she really had lost her mind, but he was the one with the problem.

"Why did you fill out an application for the shifter matchmaker if you just want to play a game?"

"I didn't fill out any application for matchmaking whatever!"

"Yes, you did!" She flipped the folder open and yanked out his application, then marched herself right into the small bathroom with him and shoved it in front of his face.

"Ramsey Nathaniel Hunt," he read aloud. "Age thirty-three, crow shifter. No family, Alpha of a crow shifter Clan, bad boy, good man."

Vina cut in primly, "And we can talk about that bad boy answer because that isn't for me. I like steady men."

Ramsey's mouth moved while he read silently, and then he yelled, "Is a B-minus in the bedroom and likes missionary style only? This isn't even my writing, and no self-respecting man would admit his shitty fucking skills."

"You cuss a lot."

"Did you not hear the part where I said this isn't my writing? It's Rike's. Sorry, lady, you've been lead on a wild goose chase, but this wild goose ain't interested. You'll have to suck someone else's dick for protection."

"For protection?" Vina asked, baffled by everything he was saying.

"Yeah, that's why you're doing this right? You look like a nice lady. A little vanilla maybe. You probably have a Suburban and live in a nice house on a nice street. You drink expensive coffee, have a few kids, and a divorce has left you bored of drinking wine alone at nights so you're looking for a fling with a mess of a man. You don't like feeling alone so you want someone around to make you feel safe from the world. Well it ain't gonna be me."

Vina's lip quivered and her eyes filled with warm tears, but she would not waste them on this awful man. With the flick of her wrist, she tossed the folder with her application on the bed. Fury fueled every word she uttered to Ramsey, "Maybe I'm vanilla, compared to you with your knives and your whiskey and your friends screwing on pool tables, but I'm still a person. I drive an old black Explorer that is on its last legs, and I have to dump half my income into it just to keep it running. My coffee is cheap. I make it myself every morning. I have no kids because I didn't find my person to start a family with. I don't drink wine. I drink margaritas. I'm not looking for a fling. I've been waiting for a crow to apply for the matchmaking service for three years. I didn't really care who the crow was, just that it was a crow I got paired with. I came in here fully prepared to give you every chance, but you aren't even polite.

"I'm leaving here feeling awful, and if I'd wanted that, I would've said yes to any of the other shifters Sarah found that matched my application. Congrats. You're anything but vanilla. That's not a compliment.

Good luck with your drinking and stabbing, Ramsey. I'm gonna go back to waiting because I've gotten really freaking good at it. And someday, one of your crows will apply for the matchmaker, and I'll make them happy because I'm good at that. I'm confident that I can make someone happy if they pick me. If they really pick me. And you're going to look back on this moment and kick yourself because I'm not half bad despite my shoes."

Ramsey narrowed his eyes and parted his full lips to say something, but she didn't want to hear it. Pursing her lips against a sob that bubbled up her throat, she bolted from the room.

She wiped her eyes as she headed for the stairs. Stupid, stupid man, and even stupider her. She'd really thought this would work. She'd just had this feeling that Ramsey was the one who was going to change her stars, who was going to turn it around for her. But he'd turned out to be a monster.

"Wait," Ramsey said, blurring past her and planting his feet right in front of her.

Vina lurched to a stop, barely avoiding running straight into him. "Move," she gritted out.

"Why a crow?"

She tried to sidle around him, but he moved in front of her again, blocking her path to the stairs...blocking her escape from him.

"Why a crow?" he repeated in a low, gritty voice. His eyes were the color of pitch again.

Vina crossed her arms over her chest and looked at the wall so he wouldn't see the stupid tears building up. "Because crows mate for life, and every boy I've ever been with has left me for someone else."

Ramsey asked, "What kind of shifter are you?"

"None of your business."

"I'll read it on your application. I'd rather you tell me, though."

"Sarah said we would be a good match because of what you said on your application."

"Like I said, Rike filled that out." He bit the bottom of his lip and shook his head with a sigh. "What did Rike say I needed?"

"Loyalty. And someone who wants a family and is protective. And a shifter who is a good future parent, and my animal...well...she will be exceptional at that."

"What's your animal?"

Vina stepped around him and stomped down the stairs. Over her shoulder she called, "I'm a moose."

THREE

Ramsey watched the woman stomp down the stairs. He'd always appreciated feisty. He was in a piss mood, and good on her for telling him off. Now, if one of his boys had done that, he would've blasted them in the face and given them a few hell-recovery days to remind them who was Alpha every time they looked in the mirror, but with Vina, all her anger had done was make him look at her a little harder.

She was cute, for a moose. Had he ever met a moose shifter? There weren't many of them in the world, and how the fuck did this one end up in the microscopic town of Corvallis? And she wanted a crow? Huh. He'd never thought about his need to mate for life as a plus for some women. Tenlee had

33

hated it.

Tenlee. Shit. His stomach curdled, and he sauntered back into his room to shower. He was going to be late to the meeting if he didn't rush. There was the folder she'd thrown on his bed. He tried to ignore it by righting a lamp, stalling. He didn't need that woman's baggage, and the hideous pink folder was probably full of it.

He picked his way around the room, tidying it quickly. He'd flipped out after that Crow Chaser left his room. She'd only frustrated him more. He needed the girls to stay away from him right now, at least until he figured out how to recover from this broken mating bond to Tenlee. But that moose...calling herself his mate... It was the most confusing thing he'd ever heard, but there had been a second, a single moment, when she was telling him he was enough just because he was a crow, that he'd felt something he hadn't felt for a long time. It was a moment of relief. A moment where his whole body didn't hurt. It was a pain-free moment where his head wasn't screaming that he was a failure.

How fucked up was that? What a mess Tenlee had left behind. He was the mess.

And that girl...that Vina...that moose? She was a total mess, too.

Brave girl, though, coming through the clubhouse. It was club members only, and no doubt she'd taken shit from the boys downstairs. Yet she'd knocked. A Nirvana song. Ha. Points for her. Too bad he would never see her again.

A wave of pain racked his body, and he doubled over with it. He barely caught the edge of the bed with one locked arm, and then he was face-to-face with that fucking sparkly neon folder. She had a hideous taste in colors. Black was the only color he didn't hate.

Cold sweat broke out on his body, and his arms shook as he grunted with the burning in his veins. His body hated him. Broken bonds were poison, and his had been so strong for Tenlee. Stupid crow. He couldn't even see when she had cringed away from him every time he tried to touch her. His animal only knew she was his and didn't care about anything else.

As long as he lived, however short that might be, he would never show affection to another woman. Women were poison. Poison to the mind, making him feel weak and inadequate, when he was the biggest, baddest crow in existence. Or he had been before Tenlee. He'd been on a path to be leader of the entire shifter culture. And now he was losing his own Clan by way of slow insanity. Women were poison to the body. All it took was sex one time that wasn't just fucking, but making love, and a man's body got addicted to that feeling. Coming was better if it was inside a girl who had his heart. But what happened when that wasn't there anymore? Strong men went to their knees.

Gritting his teeth, Ramsey opened the folder just to take his mind off the debilitating tantrum his body was throwing.

Vina Fiona Marsh. Pretty name for a pretty lady. One who didn't match him in any way, but if he was a different man, one out of the MC life, one with a steady cubicle job, weekends off, and a 401k, maybe he could've taken this matchmaking thing more seriously. She was clearly a nice girl who didn't have any idea what a bad boy really meant. He would get a sweet little thing like her killed in no time flat.

She didn't belong. Stuck out.

She was tall and curvy with long sandy-colored hair that she'd curled up real nice. Loose-fitting white

T-shirt and acid-wash shorts cuffed up high on her long legs. No visible tattoos. No rebellion at all from what he could tell. Even her sneakers had been pristine white. Made him want to make her filthy.

Wait...what?

No. He didn't need to make her filthy. He needed to leave the moose alone. There weren't many of them, but they were notorious for being extremely aggressive in their animal form. It's why they made good parents. They were one of the most protective parent shifters in existence. Fuck with their offspring and, simply put, you would die under a couple of massive hooves. Horrible way to go.

Interesting girl. Good girl in her human body, but her moose would be a monster.

He liked people who were walking contradictions. For some reason he didn't understand, Ramsey had always been drawn to the unexpected.

That girl might be a mess, but he bet she would be so much fun to ruin.

God, his crow was a demon.

Ramsey began to read her file.

Moose shifter, thirty-three years old, only

interested in crows. Parents were still paired up. Her favorite color was sparkles? What the fuck? She worked at the community center in Darby, planning events for the town. Had moved there three years ago in hopes of finding a crow mate.

Huh. What made a girl pack up and move from— he scanned the application—Michigan to come to the small town of Darby just on the off-chance she would find a crow mate? Clearly, she didn't care about love matches. She only saw one animal she wanted, and that was that.

God, this woman was something else.

She'd written an essay at the back. Ramsey ripped it off the other pages, leaving one corner shredded from where the staple had been.

Dear Sarah,

I don't really know what else to do. I hoped I would find my mate the natural way, but it's not happening, and every day is like Groundhog's Day. Have you seen that movie? I wake up, get ready, put on my make-up and dress cute because maybe today will be the day. But it never is. I go to work, I work hard, keep busy, keep my heart open in case I meet one of them in town.

One of the crows. And I have over the last year. They come here on their motorcycles, loud music blaring from some of the bikes. They go to a couple of the bars sometimes. I always hear them, and sometimes I go where they are, just on the off-chance that one will see me, and that will be that. He will pick me. I feel as if a crow is my fate, but lately, I'm starting to question whether I'm just one of those crazy girls who believes in something so thoroughly that I don't realize when my wishes have turned into something impossible. I'm lonely. I haven't been able to make friends here because none of the shifters here know I exist. They are in some kind of war. I can feel the tension. It's always been there. I've seen fights at The Gutshot that would make a normal girl nauseous. Violence is the epitome of the culture here, and I'm a rogue. No point in announcing myself until I have a shot at what I came here for. I want a crow. Even if he's flawed, I want a man to bond to my animal and actually choose me...not just pretend to in the beginning and then leave me when I'm invested. It's always the same. So here I am, eating a TV dinner on my couch, watching bad television by myself, and preparing mentally to have tomorrow be just the same as today, and yesterday, and the day before.

I need something new.

Something real and healthy. If this doesn't work, and you tell me you can't find me a crow, then I'm quitting this wish.

Thanks for trying. I know it's not easy finding matches for my animal.

Vina

The letter was dated two years ago. So she'd just been sitting here doing the same thing for two years, waiting for this matchmaker woman, Sarah, to find a crow?

Ramsey crumpled up the paper in a rush and chucked it at the trashcan in the corner. Missed, thanks to his body seizing mid-throw. It bounced off the wall and laid in a little taunting ball right be the door.

Whatever.

He wasn't it for Vina.

He wasn't it for anyone.

His crow had already made his choice.

FOUR

Ramsey jogged down the stairs, pink sparkly folder in hand, because he'd built himself up into a right rage by the time he'd gotten out of that quick five-minute readthrough. Fuck Rike for meddling in his life.

Downstairs, the Clan was gathering in the meeting room, the boys trickling in one-by-one, but Rike was behind the bar talking low to Ethan, which only pissed off Ramsey more. There was his Second and Third, probably talking about him.

"What is your job in this Clan?" Ramsey gritted out as he reached the bar.

"Uuuuuh," Ethan murmured.

"To support you?" Rike said.

41

"Then what the fuck are you actually doing?" Ramsey yelled, tossing the pink folder at Rike.

"Ow!" Rike said, red creeping up his neck. The pointy corner had hit him right in the nipple, and he winced and rubbed it as the papers rained out onto the floor behind the bar. "What the fuck is wrong with you?" He looked down at the papers, and his expression changed immediately from *what the hell* to *oh, shit.* "I can explain."

"Can you? Can you explain why you would fill out a matchmaking application with my personal information on it without my knowledge or consent?"

"I was just trying to help?"

"Like you helped by sending that Crow Chaser to me last night? When you know I've chosen a mate? I don't get you, Rike! All I need you to do is be there and make things easier while I figure out how to get over this broken bond. You're making it worse!"

"Ramsey," Ethan murmured, looking around the room at everyone gathering around them in silence. "Maybe we should talk about this outside."

"Don't you fucking do it," Ramsey snarled. "Don't treat me like I need to be controlled. I'll burn you to the ground. You think I'm naïve, don't you? You think

I don't see you gunning for Alpha?"

"Are you fucking serious?" Ethan yelled. "I don't want your rank, Ramsey! I want you to be okay."

"I want you to have his rank," Otis said from the corner, lifting two fingers. "If it's time for the vote, I vote Ethan challenges you. You're losing your mind, Ram. It ain't your fault, it's on your crow, but we all feel it. You're dragging us all down with you."

"Yeah," Dante agreed from the open doorway of the meeting room in the next room over from the bar. "We should be burying the Two Claws Clan in the woods, but instead, you sent them a herd of cattle and helped them save their ranch. That ain't how we do retaliation. You've lost your edge."

Ethan was staring at the ground, shaking his head. His nostrils flared, and his long hair twitched with the movement. "I don't want this. I don't want a vote. Nae from me."

"Nae," Rike said, glaring from Otis to Dante and back. "It's a dick-move to quit on your Alpha. You ride or die in this Clan."

"You really just mean die," Terrence said. "We rode for a long time, no questions asked, but we're watching an Alpha go weak. Ram, you can't hold this

43

Clan forever."

Ram straightened his spine and lifted his chin. "But I'll hold it today. Dante, Otis, and Terrence, outside."

"What?" Otis said. And now he showed panic because Ramsey was a fighter. He'd grown up on it, thrived on it, knew exactly what his body could do. He'd made it into a weapon. He hadn't gotten Alpha rank by default. Ramsey had fought and bled his way to the top.

"You can take my challenge," he murmured, pointing to the door, "or you can walk."

There were three beats of silence, and then Terrence, a low-ranking member muttered, "Fuck this," and stormed out of the clubhouse.

"Pussy," Rike called after him.

Otis and Dante looked at each other somberly. "Accepted," they both said in unison. Clan meant safety. Clan meant staying steady. Rogue crows did horrible alone. For stepping out of line, Otis and Dante were gonna take their licks like men. Thata boys.

Ramsey pulled his vest and T-shirt off as he followed the others outside. His knuckles already tingled to connect with their faces. Ethan wasn't coming to watch the fight, though. He followed Terrence.

"What are you doing?" Ramsey asked him.

"Punishing him for talking to you like that," Ethan murmured right before he disappeared around the corner of the clubhouse after Terrence. Lie. Ethan agreed with Terrence, and thought they should've killed every last Two Claw and dragged Tenlee back, but he needed the fight. That Blackwood blood in him required violence to stay sated. Rike was a Blackwood too, but he had more control over his murderous side.

Ramsey would hold the Clan as long as he could, but Ethan was going to take his throne when this busted bond got bad enough. Maybe Ethan was the best one to do it. Him or Rike. They'd been his boys since they were kids, barely out of high school. And those two would be the ones to kill him when he lost the Clan.

Everything had gotten so messed up.

Love was the worst.

Otis and Dante had removed their leather cuts and shirts. They were both big homegrown boys from

Kentucky. They always backed each other up, and they always took their punishment together, too. Assholes didn't know when to keep their mouths shut, but that was okay.

Ramsey needed this.

****

"What is happening?" Vina whispered to herself in the front seat of her Explorer. She'd sat out here for half an hour trying to get the courage to go back in there and apologize for her rash behavior. Sure, Ramsey deserved to be told off, but he clearly hadn't been the one to submit the application, and she felt a little guilty heaping that pile on him and then bolting.

And then there had been chaos as bikers flooded the parking lot on their deafeningly loud Harley Davidson motorcycles. The only reason she even knew what the bikes were was because there were Harley logos everywhere. The noise had scared her as the big, burly men revved their bikes and rode right past her Explorer.

She'd watched in wonder as they filed into the clubhouse, right under the sign with the bloody red crow.

She did not belong here.

Why on earth had she been so convinced that a crow was meant for her moose? It seemed so silly and irrational now. It was as if she'd built it up in her head as the only thing that would make her life okay after Jonathan had left her a few years ago. He'd cheated on her, like everyone always did, and it had been the straw that broke the camel's back. She'd just dealt with that hurt by locking her focus on the crows. But perhaps she'd just been avoiding the pain of the break-up by concentrating on something unattainable. And these crows really were that— unattainable.

Every last one of them was intimidating, and as they flooded back out of the clubhouse, she wondered for the tenth time since she'd been sitting in her ride what the hell she was doing here. How had she gotten to this moment? A matchmaker? Really? A motorcycle-riding, foul-mouthed, rebellious hellion of a man, and Alpha of the biggest, baddest Clan of crow shifters in the known world to boot? How on God's green and blue Earth had she convinced herself she could slip right into a life she knew nothing about and bond with a crow?

And holy hell, there he was. Ramsey came out

last, shirt off, jeans riding on the lowest tier of his six pack, muscles all flexed up as he talked to one of the men. His face was fierce, his eyes tar-black, and his hands were clenched in fists at his sides as he walked. Back straight, chin up, his mouth set in a thin line, Ramsey looked like a beast ready for battle. She hadn't been intimidated by him up in his room, but watching him among his people was completely different. He was king.

A king who was apparently was about to get in a fistfight, if the two opposing titans without their shirts on were any indication. They were pacing in front of Ramsey like caged predators.

What should she do? Call the police?

No. Probably definitely not. Motorcycle clubs didn't like involving the police in their affairs...right?

Whoa, Ramsey was hot. His blond hair was all spiked up everywhere, and his strides became quicker the closer to the two shirtless bruisers he got. There was a loose circle of bikers around them, but they weren't cheering or jeering like she'd seen with fights on TV. They were quiet and somber, and for the most part, were motionless other than a few who shifted their weight from side-to-side.

Half an hour ago, he'd said he was still drunk, but Ramsey was walking without swaying, and when he pointed to one of the challengers, his hand was steady, his eyes focused on his opponent. She couldn't quite hear what he said over the sound of her ovaries going *boom*.

There were onlookers in the way, so without thinking, she shoved her door open and stood up on the running board of her Ford, hanging onto the door. She could see him better from this angle. He was already fighting...or more specifically, getting his ass kicked. The two behemoths were blasting his ribs, but Ramsey wasn't defending himself. Other than his fists in front of his face, he took four hits before he backed up a couple steps. He looked crazy, eyes black as a witch's soul, body flexed, face twisted up in an empty grin that said, *Now you're fucked.*

Fast as a bullet, he blasted his fist into One's face and ducked neatly out of the way as Two took a swing. He hit One again and as he was slammed backward with the force of Ramsey's fist, the Alpha shoved the other in the chest so fast his hands blurred. And when Two went to the ground, Ramsey followed. He was on top, slamming blow after blow onto the man's face, while Two just laid there, blocking as best he could.

One ripped Ramsey backward, but whatever happened, it was so fast she couldn't understand it. Ramsey wasn't the one who hit the ground. One did. He got up fast and landed a blow right on Ramsey's jaw. The tension and silence seemed to thicken as Ramsey stood there frozen, eyes on the ground, blood pouring from his split lip. Another smile as he spat crimson onto the cracked asphalt. His lips twisted into a feral grimace as he dragged those demon-black eyes back to One. Fear flashed across One's face. Two was still on the concrete, not moving, and now One was backing up toward the wall of onlookers. Ramsey straightened and stalked him, his gait graceful like a lion with the complete confidence in his ability to kill.

There was a moment in One's expression when he looked defeated, but then he gritted his teeth as if ready to take whatever would happen. He lifted his scarred knuckles to his face, body angled, bouncing slightly on the balls of his feet, eyes black and focused like Ramsey's. They were well matched, the same height, though Ramsey's frame was packed with thicker muscle. Ramsey lifted his fists in front of his chin and angled his body, slowly circling with One. There was a low-humming, contained power that coiled tight inside of Ramsey like a cobra right before it struck... And then the fight turned to pure, unfiltered violence. Fists hit skin and faces, ribs, guts. The two titans didn't make a noise. There were no grunts of pain, only the sound of knuckles against bodies.

Vina's heart was pounding out of her chest as she clutched onto the door of her car. She'd never seen anything so horrifying in all her life. Or more illuminating. If she'd had any question whether Ramsey was a match for her, well, this put that to rest. That was a big *heck no*. She didn't understand what could've possibly happened to a man that turned him into a weapon, but she was scared to even find out. She'd been raised by a moose shifter father and a human mother, who were still together, and her childhood had been safe and quiet. But this man had been broken, put back together, broken, and put back together, over and over, changing and becoming harder and darker with each transformation until it had made him...*this*.

Ramsey was a monster. From the looks of it, all

crows were, and he was King of Crows. That's what the last line of his application had said. Nicknames: Ram, King of Crows. And he hadn't asked politely for his rank. No, that much was clear from the way he beat on One relentlessly. One fell like a tree and hit the concrete, but there was no break in the assault. Ramsey was on his knees, pummeling his face with relentless blows. She couldn't tell if the blood on his knuckles was his or belonged to One.

"Ram!" Rike yelled, his veins popping in his neck. "Enough!"

Ramsey's reaction was instant. He left One to bleed on the concrete and lurched toward Rike. He blasted him once in the face so hard the tall, black-haired man staggered backward, then fell instantly to his knees, exposing his neck. "Mercy," he barked out. Blood poured from his nose, streaming to the asphalt between his knees. He wouldn't meet Ramsey's gaze as the Alpha stood over him, shoulders heaving.

Ramsey dragged his attention to the silent murder of crow shifters who stood loosely around him. "Anyone else have anything to say?"

The others didn't answer, only shook their heads.

Rike looked over at Vina, face covered in gore, but

she couldn't understand why his eyes were pleading with her.

Ramsey followed his gaze and narrowed his glare on Vina. And then in a flash, he bunched his muscles and blasted into the air, Changing into his massive crow, leaving his jeans in a pile on the pavement.

"Caw!" he cried as he lifted into the sky, stretching his black-feathered wings to catch the air currents with powerful thrusts.

The fear thrumming through her body, dumping adrenaline into her, sealed it.

Ramsey wasn't fit for her.

Ram, the King of Crows, wasn't fit for anyone.

FIVE

In the history of the entire world, Vina was possibly the worst neighbor ever.

It was three in the morning, and she'd just laid awake for half an hour because she'd had a dream about the trashman emptying the dumpster onto her lawn. It was a horrible dream, a nightmare, because it had reminded her she'd forgotten to take the trash and recycling out to the curb last night. And so for an entire half hour, she'd laid awake thinking about the stupid trash not being at the curb. And now here she was, in an oversize T-shirt with a microbrew beer logo on the front, no pants on, her hair a mess, her feet bare, dragging the loud dumpsters behind her all the way down the cracked sidewalk of her half of the duplex.

Marsha Horbath next door was going to poop a brick when she heard this, and there was an eighty-seven percent chance Vina would get yelled at in the morning and get yet another complaint call to the landlord. But he loved her and didn't give a single care about all the whining Marsha Horbath did. He just felt compelled to call Vina to let her know what Marsha thought of her so he could go back to the the grumpy battle-ax and tell her he took care of the problem—the problem being Vina.

But she was about as stubborn as a hair in a biscuit and wasn't going to change a single thing about herself for whiny Marsha, so here she was, in the middle of the night, dragging the trash to the curb. The breeze lifted up her shirt, but hang it. No one was ever out this late. And if they were, well, maybe they would appreciate her threadbare Care Bear panties that her best friend, Michelle, had gotten her as a gag gift for her birthday but that Vina actually wore because A: she wasn't wasteful and B: it was laundry day and it was her last clean pair. They were cute and had a rainbow over her hoo-hah. And this was probably part of the reason she was still single.

Crap, the mailbox was hanging open, probably on account of her not checking it in a week, and it was stuffed with bills and junk mail. The poor metal contraption looked like a busted can of biscuits.

With a growl, she made her way quietly over the dead leaves on the sidewalk, tiptoed through the dry grass that was a few inches too overgrown for Marsha's liking, and pulled out an armload of mail. Three pieces slipped from her grasp as she made her way back to recycling, and by the time she got there, she was muttering her replacement curse words since she'd quit swearing three years ago and wasn't about to start back up now. Not for mail.

"Mother Hunker, shhhhhhhip."

Three more pieces and a magazine fell to the ground, and she squatted down right there in the street, Care Bear-clad buns hanging out, muttering to herself as she sifted through bills and junk mail and separated them into disheveled piles.

A rustling sounded above her, but she ignored it. The birds always roosted in the tree and crapped all over her Explorer. She was a bright-sides kind of girl though, so she liked to think they rested there because they liked her and bird poops were presents.

There. With a huffed breath, she gathered up the pile of magazines and coupon booklets and stood. Struggling to keep open the lid of the recycling bin, she shoved in the armload and then let the lid fall. Loudly. It was an accident. But the light still went on in Marsha's bedroom in her duplex. Whoops. *Sorry Marsha.*

More rustling, and why was she breathing heavy? She'd barely done anything physical. Hands on her hips, Vina rolled her head back and stared into the branches of the old oak tree above to find a crow.

A crow? And not just any crow, but a huge one the size of an eagle. It had a white diamond on its chest, but the rest was pitch black like the night sky. Its beak was glossy and matched the dark color of its eyes, which were trained on her.

Chills lifted the fine hairs on her arms. He was one of them. She knew that much in an instant. "Ramsey?" she asked softly, uncertain.

The monstrous bird didn't respond. He didn't move at all. He could've been one of those taxidermy ravens for all she could tell. Clearing her throat, she said it again. "Ramsey?"

Nothing.

"Ram?"

Not even a blink.

"King of Crows?"

Had he frozen like a crow-Popsicle?

"Murdery cussy fighty scary hotboy?"

Newp. Not a blink, not a breath, not a caw.

Okie dokie then. Well, giant crows weren't that terrifying when they were just sitting there politely with manners. Vina was a little lonely, and maybe the crow was too, so she sat on the curb and looked up at the stars, pretending they were watching the sky together and he wasn't creepily staring at her instead of the man in the moon.

Three minutes.

That's how long she sat out there by the trashcans in her giant threadbare T-shirt, Care Bear panties, and bare feet. Three minutes was how long she pretended to be friends with a crow before she couldn't stand the silence anymore.

Vina stood, looked up at the frozen crow one last time, and then said, "Goodnight, Ram."

And then she walked inside and left him to do crazy-crow things while she cuddled under the covers and went back to sleep.

****

Day Two.

Four a.m.

Vina frowned out the window at the crow with the white diamond on his chest. He sat on the barest branch near the bottom, nearest the trashcans she'd not-so-accidentally left out by the curb today because she was lazy and didn't feel like dragging them up to the house. And truth be told, Marsha had yelled at her this morning and called her "an irresponsible insomniatic mess." She had politely corrected her that insomniatic wasn't a word, but Marsha had only yelled louder. So perhaps Vina had also left the trashcans out there because Marsha would have to see them for the next three days as punishment for name-calling. Vina liked to think she was training manners into the woman. She was a helper.

The crow was lower in the tree than last night. It had to be Ramsey. Just had to be. She'd thought about him all day at work and looked out at the tree at least a dozen times since she'd heated up frozen taquitos in the microwave for dinner like a bachelor. Rike had no reason to come to Castle de Vina, only Ramsey.

Discovering her own manners, Vina pulled on some khaki shorts under her loose-fitting purple tank top, and even slipped on some leather flip-flops. Toting a box of chocolate Teddy Grahams, she made her way toward the tree.

"You have no reason to hang out here," she said. "I pulled my application from the matchmaker this afternoon. You're off the hook. Everyone is."

The crow cocked its head and blinked once at her.

"So...shoo. Shoo away, bird. You don't have to be here. You can go...deal drugs, run guns, assassinate people, or whatever it is your MC does. I've seen all the shows and movies, and I know you do illegal stuff."

He was frozen again. Great.

Narrowing her eyes, she huffed a breath and took out a handful of bear-shaped cookies. Crunching on them, she said, "Are you lonely? A lonely crow? I'm lonely too, so I get that. I guess if I was lonely enough, I would sit in someone's tree, too. Maybe."

Vina sat on a thick tuft of dandelions and snacked away for a couple of minutes. "I have a best friend. You do too, probably. I would guess it's Rike. He's scary, but you're the scariest. God, I hope you're

Ramsey. My bestie's name is Michelle. Michelle Corkle, but kids in school used to call her Michelle Snorkle, and she was picked on, so I got real protective. I didn't know her at first, but I decided she was my friend. Or my moose did. She's a little strange about who she latches onto. Obviously. I sat here for three freaking years waiting on a crow I never met. There was this girl in fifth grade named Lucy Maynor, and she was a total pill, used to bully everyone. But she really picked on Michelle, so one day I told her I bought her a pack of skittles and to meet me behind the bleachers after school. I beat the tar out of her and told her if she ever even looked at Michelle again, I would spend every day until we graduated high school hunting her. And I didn't even have any skittles. See? You aren't the only one who can be savage."

She giggled at herself and ate another three cookies. "Anyway, me and Michelle have been besties ever since. But she lives back in Michigan with her husband and their kids." God, her voice sounded sad. "I don't know why I just said that like it's tragic. She has a great life, and I'm so happy for her. Both of her kids are like my nieces. We meet up for lunch when I visit my parents back in my hometown." Vina scrunched up her face. "I miss when we were kids and everything was easier, you know? You went to school and did your chores, got weekends to run wild with your friends, and there weren't bills and responsibilities and failures."

Ramsey turned his head the other way and blinked again. Well, at least he was reacting tonight. Improvement.

"I've been telling Michelle and my family that I'm gonna get me a crow for so long, they don't even try to talk me out of it anymore. Finally, they gave up. Ha. And now I have to tell them how stupid I was." Her chest ached, and she pursed her lips. The cookies felt like silly putty in her throat.

Vina stood. "Goodnight, Ram."

And then she went back inside.

****

Day Three.

4 a.m.

"We have to stop meeting like this," Vina said in a seductive movie star voice. "But seriously," she said to the crow sitting on the lid of her recycling bin. "I couldn't sleep because I kept checking the time. You are like clockwork. But some of us work normal hours." She tried to sound severe, but she didn't really care. Today hadn't been so lonely.

"I'm counting these as dates," she said, testing him. Ramsey didn't fly away.

"Caw."

Huh. There was his voice. "I am. And don't try to stop me. If you keep coming here every night, I will tell everyone we are dating. And I'm traditional. I will start whining for flowers to be delivered to my place of work for special occasions and moonlight strolls in your human form." Test, test, test, but the crow stayed right where he was. Okay then. She could say whatever she wanted. Maybe he didn't understand her when he was a crow. Some shifters were like that.

"Tonight we're going to talk about my childhood hopes and dreams." She arched an eyebrow and waited, but his big wings didn't take him anywhere. "Huh. Okay..." Vina sat on her favorite tuft of dandelion weeds. Didn't matter she sat on this particular weed because she'd already squished all the fluffy white wish seeds with her bunghole last night. She didn't like killing innocent things in general, so she was sparing the other dandelions in the yard.

"Things I thought I would accomplish when I was a kid." Vina counted them off on her fingers. "Thought I would invent the flying car, but it turns out I'm not that mechanical. I mean, I'm seriously not. I've tried to fix my garage door opener for nine straight weeks now, and it still doesn't work. I've probably watched forty videos on how to fix it, and still nope. Next, totally thought I was going to marry Jake Shaw in second grade. Like...I thought he was it for me because in Mrs. Fluchey's class, we all had to stand up and say our favorite colors, and his favorite color was butterscotch yellow, just like my favorite color, so I thought we were soulmates. He has a very nice husband now, and they live in Hollywood. I'm building up your understanding of how wrong I am about most things in my life so you can fully appreciate the gem you keep visiting at nights. Three. I legit thought I was going to be a hedgehog breeder for the better part of my high school years. I was obsessed with them and their little pink hairless babies. I still want a dozen of them. Okay, it's time for my actual accomplishments. Ready? I was on the honor roll, finished four years of college for ranch management, couldn't find work after graduation, so I worked at a pretzel stand for four years, and then landed the community center gig, where I plan events for the town, and also weddings. I try not to eat my way through a gallon of ice cream at night after watching mushy couples hug and make-out and giggle all day. And truth be told, that's what I want. The giggling, the fawning, and the anniversaries, the movie dates, and the PJ parties...all of it. I want my person to find me already. I'm bored of waiting." She huffed a breath and stood. "Enough for tonight. Sleep like a log, Ram."

****

Day Four.

4 a.m.

Ramsey doubled over, resisting the urge to Change. Fuckin' crow was going insane, and he was going to hurt that poor woman, Vina. She'd looked so sad yesterday when she'd talked about wanting to find her person.

He wasn't it. Ramsey was on the fast track to hell, and that girl actually stood a chance at a normal life.

Fuck, this hurt.

The Crow was doing something bad with her. He

was visiting Vina at nights, and Ramsey didn't even realize it until these moments when he would come to, and Vina was sharing something big. Or at the end, when she told him goodnight. The Crow was pushing Ramsey out of consciousness when he was with her. At this point, he didn't even know how long he'd been visiting her. He was losing track of days, and they were beginning to blend together. She seemed comfortable with him. Too comfortable. And when The Crow did let Ramsey have consciousness in that body, it was at some illuminating moment that made him like Vina, and pity her, even more. He couldn't fuck her life up. Couldn't. Wouldn't. The Crow was a bad decision maker. He was a life-ruiner, and he needed to be stopped from whatever he was planning.

Pain, pain, pain. It was like lighting striking his body over and over.

Sweating, gritting his teeth, Ramsey slammed his fists onto the floor and buckled in on himself. He could feel The Crow, that dark-souled bastard, right under the surface of his skin, scratch-scratch-scratching to escape. But it was Ramsey's responsibility to stop this. He was the keeper of The

Crow. He had to protect innocents from himself.

Oh, he knew what The Crow was doing. He was trying to save himself from that God-awful broken bond that was poisoning him. Tenlee's bond. Ramsey retched and slammed his fist against the floor again. Fuckin' fuckin' crow. He'd never regretted being born like this until now. He'd always reveled in the power of The Crow. He'd never been alone growing up when his dad was beating the shit out of his mom. Or when his mom checked out from everything. When she'd stopped looking at Ram because he was the spitting image of that old bastard. Never alone, never lonely, because The Crow was right with him. He was right there every second, while Ramsey was fighting his way through school. Fists on skin were the only thing that made any sense. The Crow never abandoned him, even at his worst. Ramsey had always had someone right there, making him feel like everything would be all right if he just kept fighting his way out of trouble. He'd had a built in best friend. He'd never let Ramsey down until he chose Tenlee as a mate.

His crow was a brawler, but he was also a survivor. A fighter. His existence was important to him, while Ramsey was halfway to quitting life already. The Crow was watching the moose, trying to figure her out, but that would bring nothing but trouble to that poor girl. Pretty girl.

Caw.

Fuck. He was hearing his crow in his head now. He couldn't do this. Couldn't stop this. Desperate, he lurched upward and stumbled into the bathroom. No windows in here, no escape. And as Ramsey shut the door firmly and locked it, he grinned to himself at the small victory. *Good luck opening doors, Crow.*

****

Day Four.

5 a.m.

Ramsey really wasn't coming.

Typical. Men always got bored of her quickly. This one stung in ways she hadn't been prepared for, though.

Ramsey really wasn't coming.

She searched the sky for the hundredth time, but other than the twinkling stars, there was no movement.

Vina didn't want to go back to being lonely. She didn't want to go back to not having anything to look forward to. What a silly, stupid girl she was, getting attached to a flighty crow.

Her eyes burned with anger. It wasn't anger for Ramsey either. It was anger with herself that made her feel this bad. She stood, left the bright pink plastic lawn chair right where it was. She'd been so confident he would come, she'd bought this chair at the store today for their middle-of-the-night dates. She left the two beers she'd bought in the cooler too, and dragged the garbage cans back to the duplex.

She'd been a silly, stupid girl for the last time.

No more waiting for men who didn't see her for what she was. For men who outgrew her so quickly and moved on.

Pairings didn't work—at least not for her.

And forcing herself not to look again at the sky, Vina went back inside...because Ramsey really wasn't coming.

SIX

"Ram."

Ramsey squinted one eye open. His head was throbbing so hard he wanted to squeeze his eyes closed again immediately. Rike and Ethan were here, squatted down near the bathroom doorway. The floor was covered in shattered glass, and the light fixture above him had been destroyed. The shower curtain was in tatters, and the back lid of the toilet had been ripped off and lay cracked across his hip. His whole body hurt and was covered in cuts.

"What happened?" Ethan asked quietly from behind Rike. Both of their eyes were black, and they looked worried. Great. More worry. More pity.

Hoarsely, Ramsey said, "I locked myself in here."

Rike looked back at Ethan, but whatever they said with their look, Ramsey couldn't tell. "Why would you do that? Your crow wasn't ever going to react well to being trapped. Even if you were..."

"Finish it," Ramsey growled, sitting up. God, it felt like someone was battering the inside of his skull with a sledgehammer. "Even if I was what?"

"Even if you were okay." Rike sighed. "We've got bad news."

"Great. Let's hear it." Every day was fuckin' bad news, so whatever.

"Grant and Kasey got into it last night. Over something stupid. Over one of the Crow Chasers. Sabrina. Grant said something to her, and Kasey lost his shit. No reason. He doesn't even talk to her. The boys are all riled up because of...well..."

"Because I'm fucked up."

"Yeah."

"So? Crows fight all the time. If they weren't fighting, I would be worried."

Rike gave Ethan another look, and his Second stood and took over. "Kasey killed Grant."

"What?" Ramsey barked out, sitting up straighter.

"Pulled a knife on him and went to town.

71

Wouldn't stop. We had to pull him off."

"What the fuck? Why did no one wake me?"

"We looked in your room, but the light was off. We thought you were out hunting Tenlee again."

"Hunting...? No, I haven't been to Two Claws in days. At least I don't think I have." He couldn't remember much from The Crow's night flights. Ramsey scrubbed his hands over his bleary eyes. Was this really happening? And so soon? The killings? Momma Crow had told him the steps. She'd told him exactly what would happen to him and the entire Clan if he didn't bring Tenlee back in line, but he hadn't thought the killings would happen so soon. "Did he show remorse?"

"Nah," Ethan said, trouble swirling like storm clouds in his eyes. "None at all."

"Fuck! He and Grant were friends!" Ramsey couldn't wrap his head around this. He'd just talked to Grant yesterday. He'd bought Ramsey a few shots of whiskey at a bar in town and talked to him about life, about their pasts, about anything but how fucked in the head Ramsey was becoming. Grant had been relief. And now he was dead?

"Did you call the cleaner?"

"Yeah. The body is taken care of," Rike said softly. "Ram, I know you don't want to give up your rank...but we can all see it coming. We're gonna fold under you, and not everyone is going to survive it. And yeah, we're a bunch of outlaws, but we have people who depend on us, too. Grant had a son. Yeah, he's grown and lives far off, but he has to bury his dad. And we've already lost so much to Two Claws. It's like they're still here, poisoning us. You understand what I mean?"

Ramsey was staring at the glass on the floor, shaking his head. "What? No, I don't understand. Spell it out. I had a long night."

"What if we kill Tenlee?"

Ramsey was up like a shot, grabbed Rike by the throat, and slammed him against the wall so hard the drywall gave. "Don't you ever fuckin' say that to me. If she dies, you die. You understand?" he snarled in Rike's face.

"Her life," Rike choked out, "is not more important than your entire Clan's lives."

Stunned, Ramsey released his throat and backed off. He was right. She was one life and he was willing to sacrifice his people to protect one life. His. People.

The root of the problems with Red Dead Mayhem all stemmed from the broken mating bond to Ten. Everything that was happening, this storm that was building, was a direct result of Ten not bonding back. It wasn't her fault. It was his. His responsibility, it fell at the feet of his crow.

The animal had chosen wrong, and it was costing lives. Lives of outlaws and hell-raisers, sure, but there was good inside of his people. They were his Clan, the ones who had backed him while he rose to power. The ones who were killing each other because of his broken bond. The ones who were mourning the loss of their fallen brothers to Two Claws and to themselves.

This wasn't on Ten.

This was on him.

Ramsey winced at the realization. Some of his people might make it out of this alive, but some would not. And there wasn't an Alpha challenger powerful enough to best him while he still had this kind of strength and moments of lucidity. He couldn't kill Ten. Couldn't allow his people to kill her, but he couldn't let his Clan fight to the death over unstable bonds either.

He had to find a way to fix this.

Ramsey strode past Rike and Ethan and into the bedroom, and there he yanked a pair of jeans out of his closet and pulled them on, leg by leg.

"Where are you going?" Rike asked from behind him.

"To see a moose."

SEVEN

"Well, perhaps a country club would work better for what you're wanting," Vina explained to the couple. "We just don't do all that here. I can't make a dance floor that big, and you would have to bring in your own nacho cheese fountain and linens, and if you're wanting to get married in the same place as your reception, the only space we have is the empty lot next door between the buildings. I can make it as cute as I can, but I'm limited by all the brick walls. And weeds. And raccoons."

"Yeah, but I like the price of this place," the groom-to-be, Joey, told his blushing bride-to-be. She was mostly blushing because Vina had told her no on all the ridiculous stuff she wanted. No to doves being released inside the community center and no to opening a wall so they could drive a white Rolls Royce straight into the reception. And no to painting fairy tale murals on the wall of the reception room.

Days like today made Vina want to jab her eyes out with a Q-tip. Her smile was plastered as she said, "Would you like to look at the lot?"

Thunder rolled outside, but Vina was confused because the sun was clearly shining in through the windows. No, it wasn't thunder. That rumbling sound was from a motorcycle.

Out front, Ramsey eased a huge, black-on-black Harley right up the sidewalk and parked in front of the main entryway. Right there. Right on the concrete. He was breaking some serious rules! But also...Ramsey looked hot. Like...panty-melting, poontang-pounding, she-felt-like-swooning hot.

His legs were split over the seat of a low-riding motorcycle with tall handlebars. He stretched his muscular arms upward as he hit a kickstand with the heel of his riding boot. He wore ripped-up black pants, a white tank top so his ribs and the sides of his abs were on full display any time the breeze pleased. He didn't wear a helmet, and his short blond hair was mussed from the ride. She couldn't see his eyes behind the sunglasses, which only added to his mystery. Were his eyes black right now? Ramsey took off his glasses and clipped them onto the neck of his shirt. Nope. Bright blue eyes locked right onto hers through the window.

He nodded like she was one of the boys, and all she could do was clack her mouth closed like a lady and grip her clipboard tighter to her boobs.

"Is he yours?" Laura, the bride-to-be, asked.

"I wish. Wait, what? No." Vina laughed like a psychopath. "Of course he isn't mine. Look at him." She waved her hand at all his glory as he yanked open the door like the heavy contraption weighed nothing and strode toward her with the most confident strides she'd ever seen a man take. "Ha ha. Hahahahaha. Ha. No. I'm just…" Vina scrunched up her face at her clothes. It was a business suit that incased her womanly curves today. A pink one that she got from a consignment store for thirty-seven dollars.

Ramsey's worn boots made soft thuds as he came closer. He was still looking right at her. Directly at her. Just like his crow did. She couldn't even hold his gaze if she tried, so she ducked her attention again and again to the tile floor. "H-hi," she greeted him as he came to a stop in front of her.

When she cast a quick glance at him, his head was cocked and he was studying her. "What's up, man?" he said to Joey with a chin nod. "Ma'am," he greeted Laura, who'd gone all pink in the cheeks and was staring at his hundred-thousand arm tattoos with a big, dumb grin on her face.

A wave of possessiveness took Vina, and she said, "You didn't come see me last night." Oh, God. Why had she said that? She'd made it sound like he was her booty call who hadn't shown up. But ya know...Laura backed her little ho-self the F up, so whatever. *Settle down, Moose.*

Ramsey narrowed his eyes and looked from Vina to Laura and back, and now an obnoxiously sexy grin was slowly spreading across his face. "Did you miss me?"

"No!" She clutched her clipboard tighter. Her voice had held such a false note to it that her cheeks heated. "I'm not good at lying." *Stop. Talking!*

Ramsey's smile got even bigger. "Do you get breaks here?"

"Like lunch breaks? LOL, no. I eat while I'm working." Good God, she'd just said "LOL" out loud.

Laura's boot whacked rudely against Vina's. "Yep, she gets lunch breaks." Laura looked at her watch and grabbed Vina by the elbow, started ushering her toward the door. "Three-twenty p.m., it's about that time."

"I ate lunch at noon," Vina said under her breath. "And why are you pushing me?"

Was that Ramsey laughing behind them? Or Joey?

"If you don't get on that man's motorcycle, you will regret it for the rest of your life!" Laura whisper-screamed.

"But I'm not done with your tour."

"Can you give me a nacho cheese fountain?"

"No."

"Then I'm not sold. I'll find somewhere else. You have a nice day now, ya hear?" Laura had shoved Vina right to the door before Vina could struggle out of her grasp dramatically.

She straightened her pantsuit. "I don't have the right clothes to wear," she announced.

"That's fine," Ramsay said. "I'm taking you to Harley right now. I'll get you fixed up."

Vina narrowed her eyes to little squints. "I'm not dressing like those girls in your clubhouse. I'm a proper lady."

"With nice tits."

"Swoon!" Laura said.

Vina didn't even know how to respond because she was pretty sure her traitor body was begging for Ramsey wiener right now. Really? A crass sort-of-compliment made her want to hop in bed with this man? He was a rebel. A hellion. An outlaw. Sure, he had blue eyes and a million abs and really nice arms and perfect man-nipples. And look at that bright white smile. Damn, he was a looker. Probably had a big dick. His beard was on point. What was she arguing against again? Oh. "You're going to have to woo me harder than crude compliments and sexy...motorcycles."

"I'm not trying to woo you. I want to be friends who fuck."

Well, that worked for her.

"Bye Laura and Joey. I'm sorry we couldn't work out the venue for you." Vina shoved open the door and ignored the chuckles behind her. Grandly, she said, "I shall not ride this death-machine without the safety of a hel—"

Ramsey pulled a helmet from the side storage bag of his Harley and pulled it over her head, clipped it, tightened it, and then palm up, gestured for her to get on the bike first.

Right. "Uh. I don't know how to do this."

"It's like getting on a horse."

"I don't know how to do that either."

"Dear God," he muttered, but at least there was a smile in his voice. "The bike won't fall. It's on a good kickstand, and if you go from the low side, it's easier."

She marched over, took a steadying breath, straightened her helmet, and threw a leg over the seat.

Riiiiiip.

Mortified, Vina froze, leg in the air, gripping the handlebars, the heel of her black pump aimed at Ramsey's grinning face.

"Did your fancy-pants just rip?" he asked.

"Possibly."

"Date number four, I'm going to take you clothes shopping."

"I feel like you're already trying to change me."

"You can keep wearing your pink pants with the

hole in the crack if you want. Let all of Darby and Corvallis see your Care Bear panties."

"First of all, I can't believe you recognize what Care Bears are, and I kind of want to discuss that later. Second of all, I did laundry, and today my panties are pink. To match my pants."

Ramsey's eye twitched. "Get on the bike."

"Don't tell me what to do," she groused as she settled onto the back seat and rested against the leather pad. "It's rule number four on the list I gave you."

"I didn't read your rules."

"Why not?"

"Because I don't give a shit about your rules or anyone else's. We'll make our own rules."

Vina opened her mouth to argue that's not how things worked, but he'd said it with such gusto, it kinda sounded like fun, making their own rules.

"*Rule* number—"

"New word or I won't hear it," he said, slinging his leg over much more gracefully than she'd done.

"*Suggestion* number one. I left my purse in my office so we need to get back before the center closes at eight."

"Fine."

"Also, suggestion number two, noon slash real lunch was a long time ago, and I'm hungry."

"I've got you," he said as he reached back and settled her hands on his hips.

Huh. *I've got you.* That was the best three-word combination she'd ever heard. She sat there stunned as she gripped onto the side of his pants.

Ramsey balanced the motorcycle and turned it on. The engine roared to life with a deafening sound and, under her, the machine rumbled with power.

"Oh! Suggestion number three, swear not to drive fast?"

"No," Ramsey said over his shoulder. *Vrooooooooooooom!* He ripped out of there so fast she was pretty sure she left her tits back at the community center.

And what else could she do but scream? "Aaaaaaah!"

Ramsey was laughing, the jerk.

Vina clutched onto him like a parasite and hid her face against his muscular back as she tried to remember how to breathe. They had to be going a hundred miles an hour! She didn't even want to look at the world blurring by them. What if he crashed? What if they got in a wreck? Her pantsuit wouldn't protect her from road rash! For goodness sake, she couldn't even get onto the dang motorcycle without the material giving up. Her butt was cold! The wind was like a hurricane!

The scream died in her throat as she contemplated her life regrets. She didn't have a will in place, and who would inherit the savings account she had been building for her future hedgehog farm? Who would water her plants? Her parents would cry so much at her funeral.

Ramsey was saying something, but she couldn't understand him over thoughts of her own demise.

"What?" she screamed, her eyes still tightly closed and her hands clenched around his middle.

"Open your eyes."

"I'm scared."

"I've been riding since I was fourteen. I won't let anything happen to you. Open your eyes, Vina. You're missing it."

She squinted one eye open with the full intention of closing it again right away, but they were going over a bridge, and the river was beautiful. Ramsey wasn't going as fast anymore, so it wasn't as terrifying. The bridge was long. It was the one that led to the bigger cities on the other side of the mountains. How long had they been riding? When a fish jumped in the water, she gasped.

"I saw it," he said, filling her insides with butterflies by resting his hand on hers. "You can loosen up now. I broke you in."

"What do you mean you broke me in? I thought we were going to die."

"That's the scariest it gets. And look, you survived. Now we can cruise. Look around. What do you feel and see? Feel that wind? You aren't a flight shifter, so this is as close to freedom as I can get you. Relax against the back rest and take it all in."

But the touch of his hand felt too good for her to pull away. "Put both hands on the handlebars, and I will."

"I ride one-handed most of the time."

"Well I haven't had affection in three years so I'm gonna stay just like this until you stop touching me."

For a few moments, they rode like that, with his hand cupping her clenched ones right over his abs. The wind was nice now, cool, and she imagined there would be bug and bird sounds in the woods if she could have heard over the Harley. Ramsey gripped her hands once more and then put his other hand on the handlebars.

"Suggestion one," he said, barely audible over the engine noise. "Whatever happens with us, I won't ever be affectionate. No kissing or holding hands. None of that mushy shit, and it won't change with time. I had a mate. I wanted that at one point. Now I don't, and pushing me for it will make me leave."

And just like that, he sucked the breath of fresh air he'd given her back out of her lungs. He deflated her, but what could she do? He was being honest with his intentions, and all she could do was respect that.

Dominant Alphas like Ramsey didn't change. They didn't improve with time. They stubbornly stayed just as they were and didn't compromise because they didn't have to. He could have anyone.

But he was giving her this—a break from the loneliness. He'd shown up. He was letting her experience a glimpse of his world. *I've got you*. And maybe making a friend was what this was supposed to be about.

So she trusted him and relaxed back millimeter

by millimeter until her back was against the comfortable rest. She gripped the loops of his jeans and heaved a breath to expel her tension. She kept her eyes open because this right here was different from anything she'd experienced over the past three years. Maybe in her whole life. She was trusting someone else at the wheel, someone else with her life, while she just sat back and...breathed. Looked. Experienced. And she just...was.

Ramsey had really shown up.

EIGHT

Harley Davidson had huge stores. She'd assumed it would be mostly motorcycles for sale, but there were a ton of clothes to try on.

Holding up a ripped-up shirt, she asked, "Where is the rest of this? It's missing half the material."

"Just try it on and then you can complain all you want," Ramsey said as he pulled three more shirts off a rack, all in her size.

"Why would I pay full price for half the shirt?" she asked as he ushered her toward a dressing room. "And why are all the clothes you picked out black? That's my least favorite color."

There was a growl behind her, and then the rattle of a hanger before he clapped a hot pink V-neck

Harley shirt with the logo across the front in black glitter onto her pile.

"Well, the festive color is an improvement."

"Start with these. I'm going to find more," Ramsey said.

"Okay," she said. But then as he turned back at the door of the dressing room, she called out, "Wait! Do you want me to do a fashion show?"

"A fashion what?" he asked, looking nonplussed.

"You know…do you want me to show you the clothes?"

"Yeah. Fine. Fine, show me the clothes."

"And also, I'm still hungry."

Ramsey's face lit up, and he nodded. "I'm on it. Try those on." He walked away and Vina tucked her chin to her chest and stared. Whoo, that boy was fine from behind, too. Lick. He probably squatted a lot of weights. His open-sleeve tank clung to him just right to emphasize his V-shape.

Suddenly, Ramsey turned around. Vina jerked and looked away quick.

"Busted," he said.

"I don't know what you're talking about," she said and tried to shut the door in a rush behind her. Only the clothes got stuck in the door, and it bounced back open. She muttered, "holy balls," before she got the door shut again. Was that Ramsey laughing? Whatever. At least he couldn't see her cheeks turn the color of the neon shirt she held clutched to her bosom.

She pulled on a pair of skin-tight bejeweled jeans that had rips at the knees and barely scraped over her curvy thighs, but huh... She twisted left and right in the mirror. They actually fit when she got them in place. Nice and stretchy. The waist was snug, but her booty cheeks did look round and lifted in these. And the sparkles on the tooshie sure were nice. Good length to put over a pair of red pumps. A shoe box came sailing over the dressing room door and hit her in the arm. "Ow," she muttered, rubbing her elbow and staring at the clumpy black boots that had fallen out of the box.

This was the worst date ever.

Growling internally, she pulled on the boots, settled the bootcut hem of the jeans over them, and then pulled on the pink, super-fitted shirt and... *Oh my gosh*. She stared at herself in the mirror. Her mom would fall on her knees asking God why he let the devil have her daughter if she saw her in this get-up.

She should take it off right this instant.

But...her boobs looked awesome in the shirt. And the V-neck came down just low enough to show the crack between her teats. She did resemble an hourglass figure in this outfit. Her legs looked longer thanks to the thick-soled riding boots, and the sparkles on her booty glistened attractively in the fluorescent lighting. Like a fish lure. Heeeere, Ramsey Ramsey Ramseeeeey.

The door opened, and in walked her fix. She jumped and yelped then yanked her ripped pink pants from the floor and clutched them to her chest.

Ramsey shut the door behind him and started hanging up about three thousand more items of clothing.

Without turning, he reached over, yanked her pants away from her, and threw them on the ground. Then he turned to her. His eyes had been dead, but when they lighted on her, a spark of something flashed through them. As he dragged his fiery gaze down her body and back up, slowly, she felt as if he was physically touching her. His eyes went to such a dark and hungry blue, her stomach did a flip-flop.

"Holy fuck. That outfit is a yes."

"It is?"

He arched his blond brows as he nodded. "Oh, yeah. You look hot."

"I do?" she said at an uncomfortable volume.

Ramsey laughed. "Yeah. You really do. Try the black jeans on next."

"Okay." This was kinda fun. Like trying on costumes. She stood there with a big, dumb grin on her face as she waited for him to exit the dressing room.

"We ain't gettin' any younger," he assured her, crossing his arms.

"You're going to stay in here while I change?" she whispered.

"Yep."

"But..."

"But what? I'm a dude. I like tits. You have really nice ones. Take your shirt off."

Vina scoffed. "Not likely, you perverted...perverted...prick biscuit."

Ramsey narrowed his eyes. "I'm way worse than a perverted prick biscuit, Vina," he murmured as he closed the distance between them. "But this is what you signed up for, right?" He gripped her waist and pushed her back against the mirror, pressing his body to hers. "You're so wholesome and innocent, it makes me want to corrupt you." Ramsey's fierce gaze dipped to her lips in the moment right before he gripped the back of her neck and kissed her. It wasn't a gentle kiss either. His lips were hard and unmoving, and his grasp on her neck was firm.

Vina wanted to simultaneously slap him and hold him tighter.

Whatever had happened in his life to make him like this, she pitied him. And she wanted to erase the rough kiss. Wanted to change the moment. Wanted it to hurt less.

So she slid her arms around his neck and pulled him closer. She owned the dressing room kiss. Perhaps he'd done this to prove he was a monster, but that was okay. She already knew he was.

Angling her face, she sucked gently on his bottom lip. Ramsey went rigid in her arms but allowed it for a few seconds before he pulled back by an inch. The frown on his features was deep and troubled. "What are you doing?"

"What are *you* doing? You broke your own rule,

Ram" she whispered. "No affection, remember?"

Ramsey's nostrils flared as he angled his face away from hers, eyes locked on her own, a storm brewing in those dark blue eyes of his. There they stayed, sizing each other up, until he lifted her palm to his chest, rested it right over his heart, and let her feel it racing a mile a minute. And then he dropped her hand and left the dressing room. "I'll be right outside the door. Do your...fashion show."

He left her there, her back pressed against the mirror, her heartrate matching his, struggling to remember any kiss before this one.

Because something had happened. Some spark had ignited in her chest and confused and excited her. Her hands shook as she reached for the black ripped-up jeans.

That man—that wild, broken, monster of a man—had called to something inside of her. He'd woken something up. Her animal was paying attention now, and she gave a private smile because this wasn't how she'd expected any of this to go.

This is what you signed up for, right?

No.

This was better.

NINE

"You said you were going to buy me one outfit, but I have three full bags of clothes."

"So?" Ramsey asked, stuffing the bags into the leather storage compartments on the sides of his bike.

"So this is basically a new wardrobe, and it's mostly in my least favorite color."

"But how does wearing them make you feel?"

Vina stared down at her new leather riding jacket and skinny jeans and boots. "Like a bad-A."

"Like a badass?"

"Yep."

Ramsey chuckled. "I'm gonna get you to cuss like a sailor, too. Just wait."

"Why do you want to corrupt me?"

"Because you're so good and innocent and pure, and I like destroying innocent things."

"Monster."

"Atta girl, now you're starting to get it. Tonight, I'm gonna scare you off even more. Ready for it?"

"For what?"

"Club party. You'll be the guest of honor." Ramsey gallantly offered his hand to help her on the bike, but she wasn't fooled. This man was no gentleman.

Vina hesitated just a second before she slipped her palm against his and swung her leg over the bike. "When I was a kid, I got made fun of in school a little bit. I didn't care, but I learned tough lessons. One was if someone is nice to you, and it doesn't make sense that they are nice to you, be wary."

"What are you saying?"

"I'm saying if you're bringing me into your clubhouse to tease me, or trick me in any way, I'll let my animal out, and she will stomp the shit out of everyone you care about."

What was that look in his eyes? Pride? Strange. "That's sexy."

Frustrating man. "What, the fact that you got me

to cuss?"

"No," he said, placing the helmet over her head. "The fight I just saw in you. I've never seen a moose shifted, but I have a feeling yours is not one to piss off."

"No, she's not." If he even knew half of it. Maybe she should tell him. Here was *his* test since he'd been testing her all day. "When I was a kid, I had a temper problem."

"Yeah?" he asked, mounting the motorcycle and settling in front of her. "Did you beat up the other little kids?" There was teasing in his voice, and she hated it.

"Yes."

He twisted in the seat and stared at her over his shoulder. "When did you stop being aggressive?"

"In animal form?"

"Yeah."

She shrugged and settled her hands on his hips. "Never."

His brows lowered slightly, but he didn't give her grief for it. His expression didn't turn worried like Jonathan's had when she'd first tried to explain her moose.

Points for Ramsey.

And then he did one better. Before he took off, he pulled her right hand tighter around his middle and patted it. It was a silent "that's okay" that she'd never gotten from a man before. "That damage is acceptable," he seemed to say. Or perhaps he was just making sure she didn't fall off, but she was going to pretend the former because his acceptance was a very big deal to a girl like her. One who had grown up different, always making sure her human side was proper and docile to make up for the times she was a rampaging animal.

Her stomach growled, but Ramsey really did have her. Just a mile down the road, he pulled into a small dirt parking lot with a trio of food trucks, neon blue tables between them.

It was busy with a half dozen motorcycles parked on the edge of the dirt lot and twice that many cars. The tables were all full but one.

"You want to go grab that one, and I'll order for us?" he asked.

Vina unclipped the helmet from her head and got off the Harley. She was getting smoother at it already. "Uh, don't you want to know what I want?"

"No." Ramsey grinned. "I would rather figure it out on my own."

Huh. "Okay, I'll get our table," she said softly. She liked saying "our," but she would keep that little gem to herself.

He took a step toward her, and for a moment she thought he would kiss her again. But he stopped short and said, "You're different."

As he turned and walked away, she couldn't for the life of her tell if he meant that as a good or a bad thing.

Well, Ramsey sure was surprising her, too. Vina made her way to the table, helmet swinging against her thigh. He might be rough around the edges, but Ramsey had been nice for the most part today. And he'd bought her a lot of clothes and hadn't asked her to go halfsies on dinner either. Maybe it was because he knew her purse was still at the center, or perhaps he was a secret gentlemen. This man sure was interesting to try to figure out.

At the table next to hers, there were six giant men in leather vests and riding gear. She felt watched, and when she looked over at them, a couple were staring at her while the others watched Ramsey ordering at a food truck.

"Hi," she said, feeling friendly as frick. She even wiggled her fingers in a wave.

The man closest to her had his back to her but he was turned around, and his eyes were too bright a green to be human. His nostrils flared as he scented the air. "You smell like fur," he rumbled.

Red flags went off. She didn't talk about what she was. Not with humans, not with other shifters. Especially not with strangers and out in public. "Bad form," she murmured.

"You Ramsey's new old lady?" the giant, bearded gorilla of a man asked.

"Oh, I'm not that old. Only thirty-three."

The man chuckled and said, "Old lady means his girl. Are you Ramsey's girl?"

I wish. "Uuuuh, we are just hanging out."

"We figured," one of them said around a bite of a taco. "That old crow is a dead end. He can't be with a new old lady."

Vina sat up straighter. "Why not?"

"Because he's bonded. Some bitch named Tenlee has his crow, and good luck prying a crow off a mate."

Vina's blood went cold. A mate? Ramsey had a

mate?

Now Ramsey was twisted around, glaring at the men at the table beside her. He looked scary, and the table next to her went to quietly chewing their food. She could've cut the tension with a butter knife.

"Best advice," the one closest to her said so softly she almost missed it. "Run. Ramsey's whole Clan is headed for Hell. Run if you want to live."

Red flags, alarm bells, chills, all of it. Ramsey was coming this way, and the air felt too thick. A mate? He had a mate? And what did they mean about running from Ramsey to survive him? Headed for Hell? She'd thought she'd been there for years. What was happening here?

He set a buffet of food in front of them. He'd stacked a tray, and there was so much. he was looking at her with such an unamused look she was desperate to kill the silence. "Were you a waiter at a restaurant or something?"

His blond brows drew down slightly. Ramsey cast a quick glance to the next table and then back to her. "That isn't the question I thought you'd ask."

"You heard them?" she said, not bothering to lower her voice. Those bikers were shifters. She didn't know what kind they were, but all shifters had heightened awareness to people like them.

"I did," Ramsey said with a nod as he set a plastic fork and napkin neatly in front of her.

"Do you want to talk about it?"

"Do you *need* to talk about it?"

"Yes."

Ramsey shook his head and gritted his teeth so hard a muscle in his jaw twitched. He jammed a finger at the blabbermouth at the next table and said, "You're fuckin' dead, Wolf."

The man's eyes blazed and icy blue, and his lip lifted in a snarl, exposing sharp canines. Heart pounding, Vina stood with Ramsey, readying her moose to Change. Six against two was okay. A pack of wolves didn't scare her animal. The wolves stood too, and there was a loaded moment. Vina shot Ram a sideways glance, but he was smiling. "I dare you," he said, eyes sparking with excitement.

Sexy psychopath.

A soft growl rattled the wolf's chest, but he backed down. "I think Karma is already ruining you, King of Crows. I don't even have to lift a fist." He twitched his head toward the motorcycles and his

Clan walked away, leaving their trays on the table.

What the heck? As she watched them leave, she whispered, "Why would six wolves back down from you?"

"Because I'm the bigger monster here."

Adrenaline crashing, she plopped down on the bench. "Ram?"

"What?"

"Why are you here with me if you have someone else?" she asked softly.

She'd never seen a man's eyes look like his—so full of turmoil and pain. He hooked his hands on his hips and looked like he wanted to retch as he stared at the ground and murmured, "Because she'd gone. I had her, but she'd gone."

Dear God, that sounded painfully familiar. "I thought I had someone once, too."

His gaze flickered to hers. His eyes had turned black as night. "And do you like talking about it?"

"Never."

"Good." He flicked his fingers toward the cardboard containers of food. "I waited tables at an Italian restaurant for a year right out of high school. You choose first. I want to know what you like."

"But what if I choose the stuff you like? Then you will have to eat something that is not first-place best for you."

"I'll survive."

"Or…we share and eat what we like the least last."

The corner of his mouth flickered into a ghost of a smile. He studied her face for the span of two breaths before he sat down and picked up a fork. And then he tinked it against hers in a silent cheers. Or perhaps it was a silent thank you that she hadn't pushed him to talk about his mate. The relief in his eyes said as much.

She dug straight into the bison hash, but he pulled it between them and got his own bite. She liked this—sharing. She hadn't wanted to share with Jonathan, but here in the heat of the evening, with the soft murmur of talking around them and the sunset imminent on the horizon, she enjoyed sharing everything about this moment with Ram.

"How did you become Alpha of Red Dead Mayhem?" she asked low as she watched the other MC blast out of the parking lot and onto the main road.

"With bloodshed."

105

Vina scrunched up her face. "How many fights did it take you to get where you are?"

"Hundreds." He pressed his palm down flat on the table right by where she rested her left fist. His knuckles were crisscrossed with scars, and there were two new cuts on his pointer and middle.

She reached over and felt the calloused skin there with the tip of her finger. This man had seen and done very bad things. So why on earth couldn't she make herself move a single inch away from him?

"You gonna run?" he asked, as if he could read her thoughts.

"I'm not much of a runner," she said, pressing her palm over his hand.

His breath hitched and, slowly, he pulled his hand out from under hers. A rejection. It stung so badly it was hard to breathe, but she forced a smile. He didn't owe her anything.

No one did.

"How did you get where you are?" he asked around a bite.

"You mean how did I become this delightfully dysfunctional adult? Ha. Good grades in school, hard work, courses in public speaking and social skills, and four Home Economic classes."

He snorted. "We couldn't be any different if we tried. Home Ec. Does that mean you can bake?"

"I'll be baking four dozen rice krispie treats for the community center anniversary party tomorrow. It's pot luck. They always sign me up for rice krispie treats. It's kind of my party trick. I add M&Ms and chocolate chips."

The black had faded from his eyes and left only dancing bright blue. "I can tie a cherry stem with my tongue, crush a beer can on my head, am the fastest shotgunner of Bud Light in three counties, and no pie-eating contest at any state fair is safe from me. I can also make two girls come at once."

"Ramsey!" she admonished him. "Don't be vulgar. I don't want to know that stuff."

"You're cute when you're all innocent and shocked. Your cheeks get pink, and your nose squishes up like you're judging me." He lowered his voice and leaned forward. "It makes me want to fuck you until you feel dirty."

Well, if her cheeks weren't pink before, they sure as heck were now!

"For that, I'm eating the last bite." Which she did.

"Next," she said around the mouthful.

Ramsey's grin looked wicked as he pulled a container of mini gourmet hotdogs from the middle of the table toward them. "I bet you would be fun in the bedroom. All naïve, expect missionary style, and then I would turn your entire world upside down in one night. Your head would never be the same. I would get you addicted to me so fast."

Her cheeks were the temperature of the sun. Mortified, she shoved a mini hotdog into her maw.

"Eat it slower," he growled. "I like to watch you."

"I need a second," she said breathlessly. Jerkily, she stood and bounced this way and that toward a small two-stall bathroom made of old rusted panels of tin and gritty iron trim. The inside was lit by a strand of outdoor lights. She stared at her reflection in the old, flawed mirror but couldn't seem to catch her breath. He was doing something to her body, but she couldn't tell if it was good or bad. Ramsey was the most terrifying and exciting man she'd ever met.

He was also very, very dangerous. Oh, he could fight, she'd seen that, but that's not what she meant. He was dangerous to her. He was already paired up and still too interesting for his own good. He talked filthy so easily. He had lots of practice at this, was a skilled hunter, and Vina was just...Vina.

She should heed that biker's warning and run. Save herself from getting addicted, as Ram had put it, and go live a normal life where her head wasn't jaded from a man who cared nothing for a heart like hers.

But...

Maybe she wanted a change.

She huffed a breath, shook her head in the mirror at how terrified she looked, and then washed her hands just to feel the cool water on her skin. She made her way back outside, chin lifted high. She would not let him play with her like some bored cat on a mouse.

She parted her lips to say as much, but he shocked her to her toes when he looked her straight in the eye and said, "I'm sorry. I shouldn't talk to you like that. You deserve better."

The reaming she'd been prepared to give him got stuck in her throat, and she choked on the word, "W-what?"

"You ain't like the girls I'm used to." He shrugged up one shoulder. "I'm trying to decide if that's a good thing, but until I do, I should act right around you."

"Act."

"Yep, act. This isn't in my nature. I like to push people."

"But you don't want to push me?"

"Not yet."

Whatever that meant. Primly, Vina sat back down beside him. "Your gentlemanliness is accepted. As well as your apology."

Ramsey grinned a feline expression. "It was sexy watching you snarf down that hotdog, though. You'll have to open your mouth wider when you take me."

Vina's ears were now on fire. "Are you done being evil?"

"Never. But I will pretend for a while."

"Why did you fight those two men yesterday?"

Victory. She'd shocked that gloating smile off his sexy face. "That's Club business."

"Ooooh, is that how it is with Crow Chasers? You boys keep all hush-hush about everything that happens with club politics. The girls aren't allowed to know anything. Sounds like we'll never have anything interesting to talk about. I can't wait." She snarfed another mini hotdog, but this time chewed with her mouth open and stared at him, daring him to find her attractive.

He arched up one eyebrow and sighed. "Crow Chasers know better than to ask."

"Newsflash—I'm not one of them."

"No, you're not. I suspect you aren't like anyone."

Well, that was kind of flattering. She chewed with her mouth closed as a reward for him.

Ramsey pointed to a beer bottle in front of her. It matched one in front of him. "I got you a drink."

"Trying to get me liquored up?"

"They sell whiskey here. If I was trying to get you liquored up, I would be bringing you shots. Nah. This is payback for you talking to my crow." He cleared his throat and paid attention to a basket with three street tacos in it. "I wasn't so nice when you first met me, and you still look at me like I'm not a monster. I've been wanting to repay you for showing me patience when I didn't earn it."

"Another apology?"

Ramsey's Adam's apple dipped low as he swallowed hard. "Something like that."

"You're bad, aren't you?"

"Yes," he admitted low.

"It's who you are?"

Another "yes" graced his masculine lips.

"If it's who you are, you shouldn't have to apologize all the time."

Ramsey froze, mid-bite of taco. And then he chewed it slowly, studying her face with narrowed eyes. "You'll just accept me the way I am." He sounded suspicious as hell.

"Until it hurts me, yes. I'm not here to change you or mold you into a person who can match me. Live your life. Be you. Let me do the same. And if there comes a time when you hurt me with the man you are...then it's time for apologies."

"How will I know when that time comes?"

"I will cry," she told him matter-of-fact. "I never cry. If you bring me to tears, you've messed up badly."

Ramsey chewed on the side of his lip for a few seconds and then nodded. And then he leaned over to her, his face so close, for a second, she thought he would kiss her. She hoped he would. But instead, he hovered there, gaze dipping to her lips, and then he straightened again, taking her beer bottle with him. There was a chain on his jeans where a small bottle opener dangled, right near his beltloop. Like he'd done it a thousand times, Ramsey popped the bottle cap off and handed it back. And after he'd done the same for his, he did another cheers, except this time, unlike the one with their forks, he added words to the toast.

She thought they would be profound, the way he looked her so directly in the eyes, but what came out of his mouth was, "Here is a toast to bread, for without bread, there would be no toast."

Vina giggled and tinked the neck of her bottle against his. And then she took a long draw of the frosty beverage to match him.

"I think it's sexy when you eat your food like an animal," he muttered through a grin.

"Oh, zip it. I was trying to turn you off."

"Mission not accomplished."

Vina swatted him in the arm, and that's when she heard it for the first time—his laugh. It was deep and booming, and the smile that came with it was stunning. Oh, that boy had been in the mud for a while but God, his smile could light up a night.

"Are you one of them shifters?" a man in a baseball cap asked loudly from a few tables over.

The laugh died in Ramsey's throat immediately as he leveled the man with a look. When Ramsey didn't answer, the man took off his old sweaty baseball cap, tossed it on the table, and wiped his forehead with a napkin. "I asked if you were one of them shifters. The crow ones."

"I'm just trying to enjoy a meal with my girl," Ramsey said, leaning back from the table. "But if you want to row, I imagine I could rearrange your face and be back before her beer got warm."

The man spit tobacco on the ground and held up his hands in surrender. "Just an innocent question. You gotta crow patch on your vest, and your eyes keep changing colors."

The clearing went quiet as people focused their attention on Vina and Ramsey. What the heck? She knew the Two Claws Clan had outed shifters to the public, but the Darby Police Department so far had stopped it from spreading too far and wide. The video of a polar bear shifter Changing in town hadn't even made it to the mainstream media outlets yet and had been deemed a hoax by most.

"Where did you hear about crow shifters?" Vina asked him.

"You people got websites now. One of them matchmaking ones went public." The man jammed a finger at Ramsey. "That one looks like one of the guys on the website. And come to think of it, so do you."

Shocked, Vina forced her gaze back to Ramsey, but he was frowning down at his phone. "What the fuck?" he murmured.

"What's happening?"

"Drink that. We need to go."

Panicked, Vina started chugging her beer.

"Slow," Ramsey encouraged her. "You're safe."

"I'm sorry to say this," a woman said a few tables back, "but ain't none of y'all safe no more." She held up her phone to a video of a news anchor's grim face. "The news is breaking this story right now."

Ramsey's phone dinged. And dinged again. And again. Vina's vibrated in her pocket, and when she pulled it out, there was a text from her mom. *Where are you?*

Ramsey looked calm and collected as he turned his phone volume down and shoved it in his back pocket. He leaned forward on both elbows and gave her a kind smile. "Trouble can wait. Ain't nothing anyone can do to stop this now."

Vina, I'm worried. Your face is on the news. Where are you?

Her mom would start calling relentlessly if she didn't answer her. *I'm safe*, she texted, and even though this was the moment shifter lives would be changed for always, she really believed it.

Ramsey was a monster, but he'd told her with such confidence that she was safe.

Perhaps he didn't realize it yet, but he was *her* monster.

TEN(TEN)

What did a respectable lady wear to a Red Dead Mayhem party? Oh sure, all hell was breaking loose, but Vina was choosing to ignore it for one day. One day, and then she would pour over the media coverage. One day, and she would figure out exactly what the human population thought of shifters. One day just to enjoy the fun time she was having with Ramsey and the new world he'd introduced her to.

Trouble could wait. Well said. She knew trouble was at her front door, but she didn't have to let it in until tomorrow.

Today, she just wanted to have another night where she wasn't alone, eating a TV dinner, and wishing for a crow to land in her tree.

Today had been amazing, and she didn't want it tainted by the things the public said about the kind of creature she was. No, she wasn't a runner by nature, but she could ignore the crap out of a problem.

Vina tapped her chin with her pointer finger and puckered out her lips in thought as she surveyed the plethora of ripped-up ho-clothes, as she liked to refer to the garments. She'd laid them all out across her bed in a tiny hoard. Ramsey had explained the clothes looked this way because of the biker culture, which she hadn't really given much thought to when she'd sent in her application to the matchmaker. She'd focused on "crow." Not all the stuff that came along with a crow. Which, as it turned out, was a vastly different lifestyle than her current one. Was she going to have to get a tattoo?

There was this black fitted T-shirt, or this one, or this one, or the pink one, or this one over here that was black with silver sparkles. Ramsey had seemed to light up when she'd tried on the silver sparkles one. But she felt a little silly dressing in Harley stuff the first day of ever riding a motorcycle. Plus, he wasn't the boss of her. Sure, she really *really* liked the way his face went all thirsty when he looked at her in her new clothes, but she was still herself. So she marched over to the dresser and compromised.

Black skinny jeans from her new haul, but the black sparkly sandals were hers, and so was the plum-purple flowy tank top with the high neck and a ruffle around the collar.

Now she was ready for beer pong, or whatever it was those rough-and-tumble men did at a party.

Her sensitive moose hearing picked up the throaty rumble of the Harley long before Ramsey turned onto her street. She already had the tenor of his motor memorized. Vina settled the long strap of a small purse across her chest and locked the front door. But when she turned to greet him with a wave, he was frowning at the pink lawn chair she'd left in her front yard.

Was this from last night?" he asked as she approached.

"Yes."

"You waited for me to come?"

She stopped right beside his motorcycle where he stood straddled with both boots on the ground to balance the machine. No use lying to a crow. Birds saw every twitch of a face. They had pinpoint focus and paid attention. "Yes, I waited for you."

Ramsey scratched his short blond beard with his thumbnail and then crossed his arms. His tattooed biceps pushed out against the thin white cotton material of his T-shirt. His eyes looked so blue as he studied her lawn set-up. "And the beers?"

"You're making me feel pathetic," she admitted, dropping her gaze to the spiderweb cracks in the concrete.

"What are the beers for?" he asked again.

"I thought I would see if you wanted to Change and talk to me. Last night. It was nice looking forward to your visits. I got spoiled on them quick."

"You lonely?"

Vina shrugged. "Isn't everyone in some way?"

Ramsey searched her eyes, but whatever he was looking for, she hadn't a guess. "I locked myself in the bathroom last night so I wouldn't come here."

"Why did you do that? I felt silly waiting for you out here."

"I did it because I was trying to spare you."

"From what?"

Ramsey's nostrils flared slightly as he inhaled, and then he huffed a sigh. "I was trying to spare you from me."

"Because you have a mate," she said low. She'd been too chicken to ask him about it over hot dogs and bison hash at the food trucks. But this was something she did need to know. It would change the course of their relationship. She wasn't the type of girl to go after another woman's man.

"I told you she didn't have me back."

"Is she still alive?"

"Yes."

"Oh my gosh." She shook her head over and over as thoughts tumbled around in her head. "I had convinced myself she was dead, that you were a widower, because that's the only thing that made sense. Crows mate for life," she said, wanting to retch on those words because that was why she was here, and he'd already given his animal to another.

"True. I am stuck with her."

"Then why are you even here?"

"Because a selfish part of me wishes to be stuck with someone else."

Ache consumed her heart, and with the wave of pain, she took a step back. That answer felt like a blow to her heart.

"I have a mate, but I didn't matter the same to her," he murmured, settling the motorcycle on the kickstand.

"What do you mean?" The air was so thick now she was having trouble dragging in a good breath.

"You said you weren't a runner."

"But I didn't matter to someone else, Ramsey. I don't want to do that again. I don't want to be a replacement. Or second-place mate. Or some sick way to fill a void. I want to be the main event!" Okay, she was panicking.

Ramsey looked pissed. "Get on the motorcycle, Vina."

"Screw you, Ram. I'm not here to mind you. I was here to bond, nothing more."

"Nothing more? Nothing more!" he barked, dismounting the bike and stalking her step for step. "It's day one, and you're asking for everything."

"Wrong! It's day four. I've been talking to your crow all week! Investing my time already. And I was hopeful, Ram!"

He ticked his head, and his eyes turned the color of the night sky as he approached with deliberate steps. "Hope is a slippery slope, Vina."

"Stop right there!" She held out her hand. "I can't think. I can't think," she murmured. "Wait. Just...stay back. Stay there."

"Why?"

"Because when you get close to me, my head gets all messed up."

"You mean cloudy? Where you can't think about anything but what I'm saying? About my voice or every expression my face makes. Like that?"

"Yes," she said on a breath.

"That's big. So no, I ain't gonna let you push me away over something I can't do anything about. Get on the motorcycle!"

"I don't want to go to the party."

"Me either. You know what tonight is? It ain't a party, Vina. It's a celebration of life."

"What is that?"

"A funeral. And I don't want to fuckin' do it. I don't. I have to say goodbye to one of my people, and I've buried so many lately. So many. And do you know what that does to an Alpha? It guts him little by little. You know what else destroys an Alpha?"

"No."

"A broken mating bond, Vina." He swallowed

123

hard, and his pitch-black eyes pleaded with her as he repeated softly, "A broken mating bond." He sighed. "Day four. Okay, we'll count the nights you've spent with The Crow because this week I was actually able to think about something else other than the fucked-up hole I dug myself into. And I don't want to do this funeral without you. You're fun, and light, and you have this energy about you that feeds the darkness in me, makes it less...needy."

"That's not fair on me," she whispered. "I'm not just here to feed you."

"I know. So let me show you something before you shut that door on me. Let me take you somewhere I never thought I would take anyone. Somewhere I hate, but I think you need to see it to see me."

"Okay. But...we'll be late to the celebration of life."

He huffed a sigh and closed the space between them. He didn't do the knight-in-shining-armor move most men would. He didn't do the romantic thing. He didn't hug her tight to his chest and kiss her until she forgot about the red flags and sirens going off in her head.

Instead, he pushed her back against her front

door and rested his forehead against hers, gripping her shirt so tight it tugged the material lower. "You should know I'm not okay. Not even a little bit."

"Don't apologize," she whispered, closing her eyes and pressing her palms against his taut chest.

"If you can't get it in your head to be with a mated crow...I can't blame you. It ain't like with other shifters, and there will be times when you will feel like second place. And I fuckin' hate it, but this is all I have until the broken bond ruins me."

Don't cry. Don't cry. Don't cry.

"I thought I would never get Ten out of my head," he whispered low. "Not even for a second. And then you came along, and you gave me that, too."

"Gave you what."

"Hope."

Ooooh. Perhaps this was why she was here. Everything happened for a reason, and she'd been waiting and paying attention, wondering when she would figure out her place in his story. Perhaps this was the role she was supposed to play in his life. She was here for the hope of a crow. But Vina wanted more. She wanted so much more, and he couldn't give it.

So all this would be was friendship.

Friendship.

That word hurt so bad.

She'd wanted a mate to only see her, and what had she done? Fallen for a man who could only see another.

But he wasn't okay. He was asking for help, and what did she have to lose now? She could reach behind her, open the door, and let herself into her house and out of his life. Or she could be the light for his darkness until he flew away. Because he would. He'd said the bond would ruin him, and she knew about broken mating bonds. She knew about ruin. She'd been gutted, too.

Vina threw her arms around his neck and held on tight, even when he tried to ease away. "Stop it, Ram. This is all I get. This is the moment everything changes, and I want to hug a man I was starting to like before I have to pull my heart off him."

"Stop talking like that. That's not how things work. You said you were a tough girl."

"I am. You'll see now when I have to make myself see you as only a friend. My light isn't going to taste as good anymore."

Ramsey slid his arms around her ribs and crushed her to him, but there was no romantic kiss. Instead, he growled in her ear. "It'll taste better." And then he released her so fast she stumbled forward.

Ramsey strode to his bike, running his hand through his blond hair, and didn't look back. He was leaving it up to her to follow. Breath shaking, she made her way after him. And when she reached him, he had his gaze averted to the handlebars of his bike, but in his hand was offered her helmet. Another choice. Take it, or don't.

Vina gave one last look at her house...at sanctuary...at a safe place for her heart, but she was more reckless since she'd met Ramsey, and she took the helmet from him. And when she got on the motorcycle behind him, he slid his hand onto her thigh, keeping her steady as he straightened out the bike. That touch...

His hand was so warm on her leg, and here in this moment, her heart felt very unsafe, but the rest of her reached for him. And losing her mind completely, she slid her arms around his waist and laid a tiny kiss on the indentation of his spine, right between the flexed muscles of his back.

If he noticed, he didn't react. He only put his hands on the bars and gunned it away from her house. She didn't know where they were going, and as the wind whipped at her cheeks, she didn't really care. Her eyes burned with tears she wouldn't ever let fall because he shouldn't apologize for this part of himself—the part that had fallen in love with someone else and got stuck.

She knew all about that.

ELEVEN

She'd kissed him.

And it wasn't like before when Ramsey had wanted to shock her in the dressing room of Harley Davidson. Tonight, she'd been upset, and her soft brown eyes had held panic and sadness when she'd realized how messed up he really was. And still...she'd kissed him.

Just a tiny peck on his back, but she'd made the sweetest little smacking sound.

This girl was no Crow Chaser. She was real. And good down to her core. Much too good for him. Ramsey had already made up his mind to ruin her because she was time—she was sand added to his hourglass. She made him steady enough to think

129

straight, and his Clan needed him to think straight right now.

Reporters were calling the clubhouse asking for interviews, and they were about to face an uncertain future as targets. With the celebration of life and the disaster that was inside his head, Ramsey needed Vina to understand why he was going to ruin her. He wanted her to see how he'd become the monster, and hopefully...hopefully...accept him enough to stick around until he was too far gone.

He needed her time.

And yeah, he knew what he was asking of her. She'd been hurt. That much was clear from some of the things she'd said today. Maybe she'd been paired up before too, and got all messed up in the head like him. But Vina was a lone shifter who had a shot at recovery, while he was a mate-for-one-lifetime crow who was poisoning the bonds of two dozen Clan members.

Selfish asshole that he was, he wanted her to like him enough to stick around.

He turned slowly under the sign for Two Claws Ranch. This might get him killed, but the bears were fair. They wouldn't hurt Vina. She hadn't done anything wrong. And if he got shot or mauled, meh. Maybe it would be easier to end it here. Yeah, this was a long-shot, but for Vina's time...for Vina's light...for the smiles Vina gave him, he would do far worse.

He wanted to pat her little feminine hands. Hyper awareness had been something he'd rediscovered around her. Every touch sizzled against his skin. It was as if The Crow was trying to reject her hands. Sometimes it burned, like now, but a piece of him still wanted to put his hand there to reassure her he enjoyed her touch, even if it wasn't the truth.

She'd really kissed his back.

Had Ten ever voluntarily touched him or kissed him without him pleading? Never. Not once. She'd been disgusted by him, and he'd felt worthless for years. It was an odd combination for a dominant Alpha. He had to appear to have his shit together for all the men looking to him for strength, when behind closed doors, he couldn't even make his mate happy for a second. Not one second. Not once did she look at him with the dreamy look Vina sometimes did.

So why the fuck had his crow chosen Ten, and not someone like Vina?

Everything was so messed up.

"Are we in Two Claws Territory?" Vina asked over the noise of the engine.

"Yep."

"They're going to be mad we are here, aren't they?"

Vina was quick as a whip. No use lying to smart girls. "Yep."

She held on a little tighter, and he fought the urge once again to rest his hand over hers. It wouldn't do her any good for him to lead her on. All he needed was her time, not her heart.

The thought sickened him.

He wished he could be a good man who deserved her heart too, but he would never utter that thought out loud. Vina was from a different world. She was from daylight, and he was the night.

In the clearing where the Two Claws Clan lived in cabins, one big and one small, Ramsey came to a rolling stop and cut the engine.

Hairpin Trigger, the tall, musclebound grizzly shifter Alpha of this Clan, sauntered out of the barn with the Warmaker, his Second, right on his heels. Their eyes glowed bright gold. Ramsey was probably about to get more scars on his knuckles.

"If you're here to take your cattle back, fuck off," Colton, the Warmaker, called. "We sold them at auction already."

"That was a gift. I ain't here for that," Ramsey said.

"What do you want, Crow," Trigger growled.

"I need to speak with Ten."

Behind them, Kurt and Ten were standing in the barn doorway, glaring at him.

"Ten!" Trigger called without looking back over his shoulder. "Do you want to speak with Ramsey? Or do you want me to kill him for trespassing?"

"I don't want to talk," Ten called. She looked good. Happy. Cheeks all pink from the cool wind or anger, he didn't know. She was wearing a red and black plaid shirt and Wranglers tucked into a pair of cowgirl boots. She leaned against Kurt as he whispered something in her ear. Her brown eyes softened, and she called out, "But I don't want him killed either. Who's the girl?"

"I'm trying…" God, how did Ramsey even finish that sentence? With a sigh, he left it at that and repeated softer, "I'm trying."

Ten cocked her head and stared at Vina, who still had her arms clutched around him. She was shaking slightly. "You're safe," Ramsey promised her. He would kill anyone who tried to touch a hair on her head. Light deserved protection, and his soul had the scorch marks of a dozen kills. A few more wouldn't make any difference. "If you won't talk to me, will you talk to Vina?" Ramsey asked. "I know you don't owe me anything, Ten. I'm asking a lot, I know, but she doesn't understand me, and she won't be able to understand me until she talks to you."

"Are you Ramsey's girl?" Ten called, easing away from Kurt and toward them a few steps.

"I wish," Vina admitted. "He's not mine to have, though."

Goddamn, what those two words did to his insides. His entire chest constricted, and for a second, he thought The Crow would revolt and rip out of him.

Ten stood there, shifting her weight from side to side, studying Vina, then Ramsey, then Vina again. At last, she twitched her head toward the woods and took off at a brisk pace.

"Ten, you good?" Kurt asked.

"Yes," his mate said crisply.

"Good," said the tall mountain lion shifter, his eyes bright silver. "Because if you even look at her wrong, I'll use your fuckin' carcass to light a death oath on your entire Clan. And I won't stop the war, Ramsey. Not this time."

No one talked to him like that. Ramsey gritted his teeth against the urge to tell him off and beat the shit out of him, but that wasn't why he was here. He understood Kurt was protecting his mate. Ramsey would do the same thing for Vina. He frowned. If Vina was his mate. And if she needed saving. Or if someone threatened... Fuck. Ramsey shook the confusion from his head and held out his hand to help Vina off the back. But when her new boots hit the ground, a shout from Ten echoed from the woods. "You too, Ramsey. Hurry up, I ain't got all day."

God, he hated it here.

Vina walked right at his side as they made their way into Two Claws Woods. There had been a war here not so long ago. More than one. The shifters here had painted this place in the blood of the Darby Clan and several of Red Dead Mayhem as well. Ramsey fought hard not to think about that part, or he would get to lighting another death oath on the Two Claws

Clan right here. Already, he was flicking open and closed the metal lid of his Zippo lighter, a habit to calm himself down.

Ten was up ahead, but she turned abruptly at a clearing. There was a half circle of logs. "This was the first place Kurt saw my human skin," she said, looking Ramsey dead in the eyes. "I panicked because I felt like my human side was ugly. And look at me now."

"I am."

"No! Really look at me. I'm happy. I'm human most of the time now. And that ain't all." Ten lifted her chin proudly. "I gotta little baby in me now. He'll be a squirrel like me. A little brother to Gunner. Another son for Kurt. He'll be part of the heart of this place." Ten's bottom lip quivered, and her eyes filled with tears. "I'm really happy, Ramsey. Don't take that away from me."

The vision of Ten pushing that machete into her chest during the war doubled him over. Ramsey squatted down on the green grass and scrubbed his hands down his beard, searching for the steady that Vina had given him today. Ten had been prepared to kill herself rather than come back to him.

"I know," he gritted out. "I'm not trying to take your happiness. That's not why I'm here."

"Then why do I see your crow here at nights?"

Ramsey shook his head. "The Crow does his own thing now. I don't have much control anymore."

"But..." Vina said softly, her voice tainted with confusion. "He comes to me at nights."

Ten frowned. "His crow?"

Vina nodded and sat down on the grass beside Ramsey, slid her hand onto his knee, and there it was. There was that steadiness. He inhaled deeply with the relief.

"Are you fixing him?" Ten asked. Was that hope in her voice?

Ram held out a hand and said, "Don't worry about me—"

"Stupid boy," Ten said. "Of course I worry about you. I'm scared of you taking my happiness, and I'm scared you'll never find yours. I didn't want to poison you. Can't you see that? I didn't want your crow to see me as his. I waited all those years for you to see the girls who looked at you like you were everything, but your eyes went vacant around them, and you only came to life when you looked at me. I didn't want that. I wanted you to find someone else. Someone who could…"

"Care for me back," Ramsey finished her sentence grimly.

"Yeah. That."

The silence became so heavy, his chest hurt with the weight. He shouldn't have brought Vina here. This was a bad decision because she was so quiet and sad-looking beside him. She'd said she never cried. Tough girl. But her eyes were rimming with tears now. He'd messed up. He was hurting her.

"I'm sorry," he murmured to both of them.

"It's okay," Ten said, at the exact same time Vina said, "Don't you dare apologize."

Vina straightened her little spine and threw a piece of grass she'd been ripping to shreds. "Ten, I'm pissed at you."

"What?" Ramsey asked.

Ten stood there shocked, her mouse-brown eyebrows arching nearly to her hairline.

"I'm…I'm…pissed! I don't cuss, and piss is a cussword to me, but I don't care. If you only knew what you threw away…" Vina stood in a rush and dusted grass off her backseat. "Your loss is my gain.

And someday I'm going to come back here and ask you to go drinking with me. I'm gonna buy you a shot and look at pictures of your little baby and be so happy we're all okay, but right now, I'm angry. He's breaking. You get that, right? You brought out the worst in him! It's great that you're happy and everything worked out, but it didn't work out for Ramsey. And now I get to watch him—watch him—spiral! Well, F that—"

"Woman, if you're gonna rampage, rampage right," Ramsey said, standing up beside her. She was so fucking sexy right now.

"I mean...*fuck* that!" Vina was wringing her hands now and pacing. "So to answer your question...yes, I'm going to fix him. Somehow. I'm gonna make him like to touch me because right now he flinches when I do! And I'm gonna make him see me because I see him for exactly what he is! And he's hot. And sort of nice. And he's tough. And did I mention hot? And even though he probably is a little bit of a psychopath, he makes me feel safe, and I like that!" Vina spun and stomped off. She got to the tree line before she turned around and pointed a finger at Ten. Ramsey thought she would say something vile, but instead she yelled, "And congratulations on your baby. That's really good news." Her eyes were glowing a whiskey brown and looked so different when she jerked her gaze to Ramsey's. "Now, get on the motorcycle!"

And then she stomped off loudly, breaking every limb she stepped on as she disappeared into the woods.

Whaaaaat the fuuuuuuuck?

"I think she could be a biter," Ten said with a smile in her voice. "I like her."

"Me, too," he murmured as he followed behind that sexy little ball of fury.

And in a small but important victory, Ramsey didn't look back at Ten.

He only looked forward.

TWELVE

Vina needed to Change tonight.

She'd been so furious at Ten. Angry that anyone could throw Ramsey away like that. She was feeling very protective, and sometimes that wasn't a good thing with her. Sometimes it was very, very bad. Sometimes it made her moose turn into an eight-foot-tall war machine, so in order to avoid stomping the stuffing out of the next person who upset her, she should just take her destiny by the balls and let the moose have a night of running around the woods doing moose stuff.

But right now, she needed to be there for Ramsey. Funerals were really sad. And though she'd never been a part of a Clan, because moose were rare, she had researched them. Ram was Alpha, and he had little invisible bonds to each of the crows who had pledged their fealty to him. And each death snapped a bond like a rubber band and lashed against an Alpha's soul. And the pain stayed for a long time. Forever perhaps. Alphas just had to get used to pain. Though Ram looked strong and steady, the scent of ache that wafted from his skin was unmistakable. She'd never wished this before, but she would've given just about anything to take some of it upon herself and make tonight easier for him.

Ramsey cut the engine of his Harley. Vina frowned at the rock music bumping from the clubhouse so loud it shook the bike. There were three bikers outside with their arms around each other, slurring their words in a song she couldn't understand a single word of. Funerals were supposed to be sad. Apparently Crows didn't act right.

"We do celebrations of life a little differently," Ramsey explained, but she didn't miss the grimness in his voice. This night would be rough on him.

He helped her off the motorcycle and unclipped her helmet before she even got the chance to try. He dangled the helmet from the handlebar, and then he did something that shocked her into stillness. He cupped her cheeks, splayed his legs, and hunched down to eye-level. "What you did back there means more than you'll ever know."

Vina gripped his wrists to keep him there because, oh, his touch felt so good. "What did I do?"

"You stuck up for me. You had my back. You didn't think I was an idiot for bonding to someone who didn't bond back."

Vina rubbed her cheek against the palm of his hand. "I was married once."

"What?"

"Married and divorced. He was human. So you see, I know all about bonding to someone who can't bond to you back. You can't help who your heart picks."

Realization swam in his eyes, and he straightened up to his full height. "That's why you wanted a crow?"

She smiled sadly. "Getting destroyed by a man wasn't my favorite life experience. It's not exactly something I would ever want to repeat. I wanted someone to bond to me back. I wanted to be all that a man saw, but he picked someone else before he was even done with me. I was soooo replaceable, and it did something bad to my head and heart for a long time."

His eyes filled with sadness. Regret maybe. Yep, there it was. He knew he couldn't give her that just as well as she did.

Ramsey turned and walked to the side door of the clubhouse, and she followed along slowly, thinking she'd been dismissed. But when he got there, he opened it wide and waited just inside the open frame, his eyes darkening like storm clouds but holding steady on her. And when she said "thank you," and passed through, he pulled her to a stop by the arm, gripped the back of her neck roughly, and then kissed her so hard his teeth made her bottom lip throb. She stumbled back a step when he released her from the kiss, but his grasp in the back of her hair brought her close again. Inches away from her face, he growled, "If anyone in here lays a hand on you, tell me, and I'll deal with them."

Muddy-minded, she murmured, "Maybe I'll find my real mate tonight."

His eyes morphed to black. He gripped her waist and gave her the devil's smile. "No, you won't, and it's best if you don't joke like that with me."

"I thought we were just friends," she popped off as he walked away.

"Go ahead and test that theory, Vina, and see whose face I smash tonight."

And there were those butterflies in her stomach, and there was that smile on her face, and there was that feeling she was getting addicted to—hope.

Possessive man. That's what she needed. Not the wishy-washy *maybe I like you, maybe I don't.* She needed a man to point at her in a crowd and say, "That's mine. She's under my protection. Everyone else fuck off."

Jonathan had never once stuck up for her or protected her from overzealous boys when they were out. And there had been many of those situations since he never acted like he was with her, so she looked single. She'd always had to get herself out of uncomfortable spots. He'd never cared enough. But Ramsey—big, dominant King of Crows—had just told her she was his. And he was willing to reprimand his own people if they crossed a line.

Safe.

Safe.

Safe.

145

The second she walked in, she stuck out like a sore thumb. Along the bar, intermingling with the burly bikers, were four Crow Chasers in shredded black tank tops and T-shirts and high heels she'd only seen on strippers in movies. And there was a moment when she paused in the entryway that she knew, without a shadow of a doubt, she did not belong here.

But then she saw Ramsey. He was a few yards ahead of her, watching her reaction, his eyes such a vivid blue now they looked unreal. There had been so many times when she'd had the opportunity to bolt, not dig into his life deeper, but just like all the other times, she took a step forward instead of a step back. With a shy smile, she stretched her fingertips for his offered hand. He didn't hold onto her long, just enough to get her moving toward the bar. A few seconds of warmth, and then he released her hand and made his way to a cluster of bikers greeting him. They were all manly hugs and gritty-voiced hellos. The dynamic here was unexplainable. It was happy and somber all at once. It was relief that their Alpha was here, but with undertones of discomfort, too. There was something in the air she couldn't describe, and it left the fine hairs on her forearms electrified.

"Hey there, Soccer Mom, where's your gift?" Rike asked as she sat in a stool at the bar near a couple of the Crow Chasers.

Vina looked around but didn't see anyone else with presents. "What gift?"

"At a celebration of life for crows, it's customary for strangers to bring a gift for the mate of the deceased." His dark eyes softened. "And if the crow is unpaired, like Grant, like all of us, you bring a gift to the best friend."

Vina's heart sank to her toes. "Who is...?" She cleared her throat and corrected herself. "Who *was* Grant's best friend?"

Rike pointed to a man alone in the darkest corner of the room, sitting in an old chair, elbows on his knees, hunched forward, staring with an unreadable expression at where Ramsey was greeting his Clan, strangling the neck of a half-empty beer bottle he held in his hands. "Grant's best friend is his murderer. That's Kasey."

"Oh, my gosh. He murdered him? Why?"

"Get used to it, Soccer Mom," Rike said grimly. "We will all be murderers by the time our caskets drop."

"Why? Because you are all bad? I don't believe that."

Rike shoved a shot of what smelled like cheap whiskey across the bar counter at her. "Ain't no good men in this Clan, so get that out of your head right fuckin' now. We're all headed to Hell. Ramsey is just leading us there a little faster than planned." He turned to a tall man with long hair and brown eyes like Rike's. He was sitting a few chairs down from her. Their features were similar. Maybe they were brothers. "What can I get you, *Second.*" The way he said the last word sounded like a cuss word it was spat with such vitriol.

"Don't start shit with me tonight, *Third,*" the man said in a soft growl. "You know I don't want to be in this position. Give me the bottle."

"Fuck you, Ethan. Get your own bottle." Rike gritted his teeth and looked like he wanted to spit. His soft brown eyes had turned black.

Ethan pointed to Vina. "She shouldn't be here. Red Dead Mayhem only tonight."

"Yet you let the Chasers right in, and ain't none of them Mayhem."

Ethan slammed his fist on the bar and leaned

closer to Rike. "So you think it's a good idea for her to see what's happening?"

"She's a shifter," Rike said with a shrug and gave Ethan his back before he began to dry wet glasses near a sink against the wall.

"What's happening?" Vina asked.

"None of your fuckin' business, Normie," a blond with painted red lipstick to match her red nails gritted out from a couple chairs down. She looked mad as hell. What was wrong with her? Vina had never even talked to this girl.

"I'm not a Normie, whatever that is."

"Well, you ain't one of us."

"What the fuck is the problem?" Ramsey asked from across the room where he'd migrated to talk to Kasey. His black eyes locked on the Crow Chaser, then Rike, then Ethan, and lastly, Vina. "Have some manners around Vina, or you can leave. In fact, Hannah?" Ramsey pointed to the door. "You can see your way out. Your presence here isn't necessary tonight."

"You didn't think I was unnecessary when I blew you in the bathroom."

"Oooooh," some of the men jeered.

Ram straightened his spine and stalked toward Hannah, but the stupid Chaser didn't duck her gaze or back off. She stood and crossed her little arms over her big chest. "I have every right to be here, Ram. If I'm good enough to suck your dick, I'm good enough to stay for a celebration of life. I have way more right than this bitch."

Red fury sizzled up Vina's spine. Jealousy and rage warred in her, and she clenched her fists on the bar top, barely resisting the urge to split the Chaser's lip for calling names. For touching her Ramsey. Her Ramsey. Hers. Vina jerked her gaze from the blond hellcat and leveled Ram with a look.

"Two years ago," he said simply.

Didn't matter if he fooled around with this woman twenty years ago. Vina wanted to put a hoof through her face anyway just for bringing it up.

"Your eyes look freaky," Rike said to Vina. Was that a smile in his voice? "Mostly dark gold with a thin whiskey rim. They glow on the outsides. What color do yours turn, Hannah? Oh wait, they don't turn because you're the fuckin' Normie around here."

Hannah huffed a breath. Two of the other Crow Chasers, two brunettes, click-clacked toward her.

"You gonna piss on the girls who keep you and the boys happy?" the shorter brunette asked, venom in her voice.

"Yeah, Rike," Ethan said. "You gonna take this stranger's side over the girls who have been loyal for years?"

"I ain't takin' sides, Second. Or if I am, it's Ramsey's side. He brought a girl. A good one. A fuckin' soccer mom, not some ho lookin' to suck off a crow for attention. Good on him. And bonus, Vina ain't the Origin." Rike spat on the floor, and when he looked slowly back at Ethan, his eyes were black. "At least he's got enough faith in himself to try to save us."

"He ain't saving shit, and you and everyone here knows it," came a slow, steady drawl from the other side of the room. Kasey. His eyes matched the shadows he sat in, but his hate-filled glare was trained on Ramsey, who had come to lean on the bar and watch the arguing with a suspicious frown on his face.

"This a coup?" Ram asked slowly. His voice sounded terrifying, as if he'd come from the depths of hell.

There was something different in the air. Some dark power that made Vina want to curl into herself and retch. Was this what evil felt like?

No one answered the Alpha, so he flexed his broad shoulders, held his hands out to his sides and demanded louder, "Is this a coup?"

The others were gathering closer now, like hyenas on a lion kill. All eyes were black. All souls felt black. Vina swallowed hard, stood slowly, and inched toward Ramsey's side. It wasn't so he could keep her safe. No, it was because she would unleash Hell if they warred.

"Oh, what are you gonna do, cow?" Hannah asked. "That's what girl mooses are called, right? Cows? You gonna run around and break shit? These are crows. You have no business in the ranks here."

Vina gave her an empty smile. "It's moose, you bimbo."

"What?"

"The plural isn't mooses. It's just moose. And yeah, I guess I'm pretty good at 'breaking shit.'" She used air quotes on that. "'Shit' being people like you. Take one more step toward me, and I'll escort you out of here myself."

Hannah laughed and looked around at the men still creeping closer to Ramsey. "He can't protect you. He made everyone like this. You know what a Clan of crows is called, Normie? A murder of crows. And Ramsey made them all murderers with his bad decisions."

"Mmm," Ramsey said, his chin high, watching his Clan advance. "Something tells me Vina didn't pick me for protection, though she has it. Y'all wanna fight?"

"Yep," Kasey said, making his way through the crowd. "There's blood on my hands because of you. I woke up standing over my best friend. I woke—" He choked on the last word. "Where did I go? Where do we all keep going? You think you're the only one who blacks out and flies to Two Claws Woods? You're the only one sleep-flying?" Face turning crimson, Kasey screamed, "Wrong! You're killing us all." His voice dipped to a whisper. "One by one, you'll kill us all. And for what? Love? Get a grip, Alpha. Love is poison. Same shit you've been preaching your entire rise to the top. We got no mates because you said no, but you go and choose the worst one, some squirrel bitch who doesn't even care about you back. Some legendary Alpha you are." Kasey pointed a finger at Ethan. "Challenge him. Kill him. I'm already in hell— I'll be haunted by Grant." He twitched his head to the corner where he'd been sitting in the shadows. "He's sitting over there right now, eyes on me. Always on me. Empty eyes. Bleeding everywhere. Can you see him?"

Chills rippled up Vina's arms as she glanced at the dark corner with the empty barstool. Nothing was there except that awful dark feeling.

"Yes, I see him," Ramsey said. "I see all of them."

The hate in Kasey's glare faltered.

"What?" Rike asked, making his way around the bar to stand beside Ramsey. "All of who?"

"Every crow who has ever bonded to me and died in my Clan. Every life I've taken. He jerked his chin toward Grant's corner. "Grant." He gestured to the pool table. "Barret, Noel, Hatchet, Wright." He jammed a thumb behind him. "Bentley likes to watch me from behind the bar. Thorn is always in the bathroom. The woods outside? Every crow who has lost a challenge to me over the past fifteen years. Congratu-fucking-lations, Kasey. You get to see your first ghost." Ram cocked his head in a bird-like manner. "I see dozens. I'm never alone. I'm never at peace. Some Alpha I am? Where were you when you came to me? Strung out on meth, alone, no protection, you'd pissed off an entire MC, couldn't even ride your Harley ten feet without laying it down, and what did I do?"

Kasey took a step back and looked uncertain.

"Say it or I will," Rike gritted out from Ramsey's other side.

"What did I do?" Ramsey yelled suddenly, filling the entire bar with his commanding presence.

Kasey swallowed hard and dipped his gaze to the scratched-up wood floors. "You killed the men who were after me and my kid."

"Why did I do that?"

"Because..."

"Why?" Ramsey demanded louder.

"Because you said you saw something in me worth saving. You said my boy deserved to have me here."

Ramsey jammed his finger over to Grant's corner. "Do you know who stands with Grant?"

Kasey squeezed his eyes tightly closed as he shook his head. "The Daybreaker Clan?"

"And have I ever made you feel bad for that? Have I ever laid the burden of what I did for you at your feet, Kasey?"

Kasey ran his hand down his face and then wiped the palm of his hand on his jeans. He sniffed and shook his head.

"I'm watching your little boy grow up with his dad around, and now ask me Kasey. Ask me if I would do it again. Ask me if I knew then what I know now, that I would be haunted by them, would I still see the potential in you? Would I still kill 'em?"

Shaking his head, Kasey ran his hands back and forth over his hair. His shoulders were shaking. He tried and failed to get a single word out. Finally, he croaked out, "I killed him. I killed Grant. I was so mad. So mad and I couldn't stop."

Ram pulled him in suddenly, clapped him on the back so hard the bar echoed with the sound. "Grant's blood ain't on your hands, Kasey. It's on mine. Look at him now. Who is he looking at?"

When Kasey turned to the corner, Vina could see a single tear streak down this big, burly man's cheek. "He's lookin' at you."

"Let him go, Kasey. He's my ghost now. I'll take

'em all to save y'all pain. They're all mine."

Vina was crying. She couldn't help it. She'd just got a peek at the raw. She'd just witnessed part of what made Ramsey the Alpha of all Alphas for the crows. He sacrificed himself daily but had never voiced it until now. Vina reached in her pocket and pulled out her old, tarnished lucky penny with the heart cut out of the middle. With a sniff, she formally said to Kasey, "Crow, my dad gave this to me when I moved out and told me it was lucky. I've carried it in my pocket all this time." She squeezed the penny one last time just to feel the comfort of it. How many times had she held it in painful moments? She closed the three steps between them just as Ramsey released Kasey from his embrace. And then she held it out on her palm. This was her offering to the best friend of the deceased.

Kasey stared at it with shock in his black eyes. He glanced up at her, his head cocked, and then back to the penny. Swallowing hard, he took it gently from her palm and nodded once, slightly. His eyes were full of phantoms as he met her gaze again. "You gonna save us all, Normie?" he asked softly.

She wished she could say yes. She wished so hard,

but she wasn't a liar. Ram was bonded to another. The one who could save them was happily nestled with her mate in the Two Claws Clan. "My name is Vina."

A woman's booming voice sounded from the stairway. "Give your gifts, and then let's do this celebration of life up right. Grant deserves it." She was statuesque and straight-spined, dark hair with blond streaks, perhaps in her mid-fifties or early sixties. "Ladies, you all need to leave. Ramsey already told you this is Clan only."

"Leave forever?" Hannah's voice pitched up in a whiny tone.

"Ask one more fuckin' question, Hannah, and yes, I will ban you forever," Ramsey growled.

"Fine." She grabbed the short brunette's hand and then Vina's hand and yanked them toward the door.

Rage rippled up her spine, and Vina nearly yanked that little tramp's arm out of its socket escaping her grip. Hannah's nails scratched deeply into her wrist, but Vina didn't care. Her hand was on the wench's throat and her fist was already poised, reared back, ready. God, her moose was right there, ready to stomp this little hellion into a smear on the floor.

A big strong hand cupped her fist and stopped her progress. There was a smile in Ramsey's voice when he told Hannah, "Touch her again, and I won't stop her from rearranging your face next time. I'd bet my flight feathers *mooses* are tougher than fragile-necked little Crow Chasers."

Hannah was making little choking sounds and staring in shock at Vina's fist all wrapped up in Ramsey's. Vina released her throat slowly. It would've been so easy to pop her stupid little head from her neck. Geez, she needed to Change soon. Her rage was too easy to access right now. "I've got a little temper problem," she admitted. "Perhaps stop testing it. I'll leave here on my own."

"Nah," Ramsey murmured, pulling her fist to his lips. He kissed her knuckles in the gentlest gesture a monster could make. "Vina stays. She's my shot at burning that damaged mating bond. Until I dig out or you boys have to put me down? She's my lady. I ain't quittin' yet, but I need help. Can't do this on my own, as much as I want to. I need the Clan. I need this girl. I need time. I need to rip this goddamn broken heart out of my chest and grow another one, and until I figure out how to do that? Vina is queen. Let her try and save me." He looked over at Rike. "Shots for Grant. You know what he liked."

"Jameson!" the boys yelled in unison.

Rike was already behind the bar pouring the amber liquor into a huge row of shot glasses, and there was a surge of big burly bodies toward the booze.

Ramsey held her back when Vina moved to follow them. "You're a good surprise," he murmured against her ear as he intertwined his fingers with hers.

She squeezed him back and closed her eyes at how good his touch felt. "I thought you said no handholding."

"Rules are made to be broken, Vina. You should know that I'm going to be terrible at this. I won't pay attention when I should, be as sensitive as I should, or understand your girl shit. But I can promise I'll keep you safe, and I'll do my best to keep you happy while I'm here."

"That's the prettiest promise I've ever heard."

Ramsey sipped her lips. She didn't know how long they stood like that, just pressed against each other. It was the sweetest moment of her life, holding hands with a boy who was capable of inflicting great pain on other men who threatened him or his people, but who touched her like she had butterfly wings. His lips moved against hers, and the chaos around them died to nothing. All she could hear—the only thing— was the beating of their hearts. They raced each other. Ramsey pulled back with a soft smack of his lips and then nipped at her neck. "Woman, you almost clocked that Crow Chaser." Yep, that was definitely a smile in his voice.

"Yes, I did," she said. Her moose sure as heck wasn't going to stop her fist. If Ramsey hadn't been there, Hannah would've had a crooked nose to give her face a little more character.

Ramsey's voice softened to a whisper. "And you gave Kasey your penny. I don't think anyone has ever shocked me so much in a single day in my whole life. Stay with me until the end."

"What?" she asked, easing back.

Ramsey searched her eyes. She hated the sadness in the ocean blue of his.

He said, "You make things easier. Stay until they have to put me down. I know it ain't fair of me to ask, but I'm selfish."

"You said you weren't giving up."

He offered her a slow, crooked smile. "First rule of being Alpha, never show your Clan weakness."

And as he turned and walked toward the cluster of crows at the bar, singing some Irish drinking song she'd never heard before, she allowed a little private smile.

Kasey's hollow voice echoed in her head. *You gonna save us all?* This was the moment she decided that answer. She didn't have to save them all, just Ramsey, and he was strong enough to do the rest.

First rule of being Alpha...

In the words of the King of Crows... *Rules were made to be broken.*

THIRTEEN

Vina was doing something to him. Something Ramsey didn't understand, something he couldn't comprehend, something he couldn't explain if he sat there for hours and tried.

Ramsey sat back in his creaking chair at the bar as he watched Vina play pool—quite terribly, if he was honest—with Decker. A few of the others were hanging around, giving her shit, calling her Soccer Mom and Queena, which was the combo of queen and Vina that one of the drunk crows had come up with in a moment of genius. She was taking the nicknames in stride, though. She could take a joke. Test passed, because in this clubhouse, that's what they did. They gave each other shit and they dished it back and they moved on.

"She's something else," Rike said from behind him.

Ramsey turned to see his Third wiping down the counter with a white rag.

"Yeah, she's shit at pool. Remind me never to play doubles on her team," Ramsey teased.

"Ha. There it is."

Ramsey frowned. "There what is?"

"One of the first genuine smiles I've seen on you in four years. You been wearin' it a lot tonight while you sit over here like a creeper watching your mate."

"My mate? Nah." He stared at Vina. "Four years?" Ramsey asked softly.

Rike sighed and leaned on his elbows on the bar, nodding his head. "Kasey was right. You did preach about love being poison, and it was. For you. And for us who had to watch Tenlee hurt you, and feel the aftereffects, it was poison too. Tenlee? She didn't ever belong here. Your crow fucked up when he picked her." His dark eyes scanned to where Vina was leaning over the pool table, lining up a shot into the corner pocket that no one could possibly miss. She missed. She laughed, her giggle sounding clear like a bell in contrast to the gritty laughter from the boys. Rike gave Ram a crooked smile. "The soccer mom fits better. You know what I saw tonight?"

"What?"

"I saw you kiss her over there when I was pouring shots. I saw you kiss Tenlee dozens of times, and it was always the same. She pulled away. She flinched away from your touch. She looked sad, uncomfortable, and I know you felt that rejection every time you touched her. I could see it on your face, too. That's like your heart getting whipped for years, Ram. I thought you'd be ruined from it. Never want to touch a girl again unless you were fucking her, no emotions. But tonight?" Rike twitched his head at Vina. "That girl leaned into you like there was no one else in the whole world but you two. She was stiff when she came in here, tense, and you melted her to fit right against you. And when you pulled away, she had this smile that lingered and hasn't gone away yet. Look at her."

Ram dragged his attention to Vina, and their gazes collided. She looked away quick, cheeks turning a pretty color of pink at being busted staring at him. That smile Rike talked about was right there, curving her full lips, as she snuck him another shy, sideways glance.

"She can't help lookin' at you," Rike said. "Been doin' it all night like she misses you, and you're sitting right here."

"Don't mean she belongs," Ethan said from a few chairs down. His long hair hid the side of his face, but he seemed to be looking at Vina, too. Ram had this instant urge to grab the back of his hair and slam his face onto the bar just for lookin' dirty at his mate. Errr...his girl. Mate was the wrong word. It had jumped into his head because Rike just used the term. That's all. Fuck. Everything was confusing. And that made him want to pummel Ethan even more.

"Maybe it's you who doesn't belong," Ramsey said. He let his words stay cool, but under his skin, his blood was boiling hot.

Ethan took a long swig of his beer and slammed it on the counter, then stood and sauntered toward the pool table.

"Watch your step," Ramsey warned him.

"Or what?" Ethan asked, turning and walking backward with a devil-may-care smile.

"Or I'll put you in the corner with the rest of the

ghosts." And he fuckin' meant it. Oh, he knew what had almost happened tonight. Trouble had been brewing in the Clan for a while, and Ethan wasn't acting right. He'd been closed off. Stopped talking openly to Ramsey. He had the others in his head, telling him to challenge Ramsey for the Clan and save them all. At the cost of Ramsey. Well, he could've fuckin' tried tonight, and Ethan would've died for it. So what if he was pissed his little coup didn't happen? He could've still thrown down an Alpha Challenge. He could whenever he wanted to. If he pushed Ramsey too much, Ramsey would call an Alpha Challenge himself and put Ethan squarely in his place. Under Rike this time. Maybe at the bottom of the fuckin' Clan just to make an example of him.

Ethan wasn't stupid, though. He knew Ramsey would do that without hesitation. It's why he hadn't Challenged him earlier. He was treading a thin line now. Letting his anger build. The Clan had put that hunger for power in his head. Ramsey knew all about that. He'd fought for his place at the top of the crows so the power could feed his insatiable appetite. Ramsey didn't trust his Second anymore. Tonight was a celebration of life. It wasn't a time for messing with the pecking order of the MC. The focus needed to be on Grant's passing. Tonight honored a fallen crow.

Tomorrow Ramsey would deal with Ethan and get his Clan back in line.

If he was sane enough. God, Vina had her work cut out for her.

The smile fell from Vina's lips as Ethan whispered something into her ear. The light dimmed from her eyes. She gripped her pool stick like she wanted to blast it against Ethan's face.

Ram didn't know what pissed him off more: Ethan stealing Vina's good night or that his lips were close to his girl. In the shadows, the ghosts were restless, as if they could feel the darkness building inside of Ram.

Ethan was playing a dangerous game and building a storm. The broken mating bond to Tenlee felt like nothing more than a brush against his soul compared to the black fury that was consuming Ram as he watched Ethan ease away from Vina with a wicked smile on his lips.

****

"You'll never belong here. Never with him. He'll always be bigger than you," Ethan murmured in

Vina's ear.

"Ethan, back off," Kasey murmured from his place against the wall. He looked exhausted, his eyes sunken in, as though he'd aged ten years tonight.

"You should know your place here," Ethan told her. "You rank somewhere under the cockroaches. And when you walk out of here crying because you've been demolished, I'll have warned you. Crows feed on lesser shifters like you. Ram might be king, but you ain't no queen."

Something shiny and silver flew past her so fast she gasped and lurched back.

Thud! The knife hit the wall behind them at the same time Ethan yelled, "Fuck!" and flinched toward her. He put his hand to his cheek, and when he pulled it away, his fingers were smeared with crimson.

At the bar, Ram stood leaning against the bar top on his elbows, chin lifted high, eyes black as night and trained on Ethan. "I told you to watch your step. That's your warning. I won't miss on the next one."

Rike stood frozen, just behind Ram on the other side of the bar, eyes round, mouth hanging open.

Ethan glared at his Alpha for a few loaded moments and then cast Vina a furious glare. Blood streamed down his jawline on his left side.

"Well, that's gonna leave a mark," she muttered.

Behind her, a couple of the boys snickered. Ethan bowed low, his eyes never leaving hers. "Queen," he gritted out. Then he spun on his heel and made his way out the front door, red polka-dotting the floor in a trail behind him. The door slammed, and a second later, the roar of a Harley engine rumbled.

Then he was gone, and Ramsey was headed her way, looking like pure fury. Uh oh.

"What did I do?" she asked as she set the pool stick on the table.

"It's what you're gonna do that matters, Vina," Ramsey snarled. "Night boys."

"Good luck," Kasey called as Ram led her toward the stairs by an unbreakable grip on her hand. Whether he was talking to Vina or Ram, she couldn't tell.

There was a heaviness roiling around Ramsey and making it nearly impossible to breathe. By the time they reached the top of the stairs, she was gasping for breath, and her entire body felt like it wanted to freeze in place.

She made it all the way to the top of the stairs

before she eased out of his grasp. "Ram, are you okay?"

He didn't answer. Instead, he turned on her. He gripped her waist with one hand, the other cupping her neck as he pushed her back against the wall. With anyone else, she would've fought being trapped against a wall by a dominant. But with Ram, it was just him. Rough boy when he was in the heat of the moment. The kiss on her lips was volatile, but she loved it. He wasn't hiding who he was, or gentling down to coddle her. He was asking her to accept him as is. His mouth moved against hers with the force of a hurricane and the desperation of some wild animal cornered and hurt. His grip on her tightened the second she let off a little needy moan, and he rolled his pelvis against hers. His big, hard erection was right there, separated from her skin by only a few layers of clothing. This wasn't how she'd imagined sex with a crow would happen. It wasn't in her rules. This was unpredictable, just like Ram, and in that moment, she knew it would always be like this. She could fight it and cling to her rules on how lovemaking should go with her, or she could put it in his hands and accept the man she was falling in love with for all of his unpredictable ways.

Ram picked her up, pushed her back against the wall again, and ground his hips between her legs. Vina threw her head back and closed her eyes as his lips went to her throat. His whiskers were rough against her sensitive skin there, but it felt so good. She was revved up, she could finish just like this, clothes on with him rubbing against her.

"Who do you belong to?" he ground out against her neck.

"No one," she growled stubbornly.

"Wrong answer." He yanked her off the wall but didn't put her down. Instead, he walked with her wrapped around him toward the last door at the end of the hallway like she weighed nothing at all. Vina gripped the back of his neck to stay in place, and when he kicked the door to his bedroom closed behind them, she reached for the light switch to turn it off.

"Nope," he growled, intertwining one hand with her outstretched fingers.

"But the lights are on," she pointed out breathlessly.

"I'm not fucking you in the dark, Vina. I wanna see

your body."

"But...but..." She was supposed to fight this part though, right? Because she wasn't super-confident about what she looked like naked, she was supposed to argue for the lights being off. At least for the first twenty times?

Ram dumped her on the mattress, and she bounced once with a squeak. Argument time! But when she parted her lips to give him what for, Ram stood over her, removing his shirt and, oh my good green plant life in the spring, the man was fine.

Vina lay there like a stunned starfish staring at his flexing eight-pack. Tattoos—yes, biceps—delicious, shoulders—broader than a barn door, smile...utterly wicked.

She went to close her legs, embarrassed by how much her body was already reacting to him, but he reached forward and shoved her knees back apart and shook his head slowly.

Hot. Man.

This was like a book! Or like a movie. Like one of those sexy movies where the couple was cool and coordinated, except she was a clumsy good-girl nerd who knew not what she was doing in the bedroom.

Apparently, Ramsey had this though, so now was the time. No arguing for the lights, she should just enjoy this. And forget what Stupid Ethan said about her not belonging with Ram. The King of Crows apparently felt differently because he was definitely unbuttoning his jeans. Was she supposed to take her clothes off now? Yes! Absolutely probably she should. She sat up to struggle out of her blouse, but it had a zipper in back, and she wasn't looking that sexy as she struggled with it.

Ram straddled her, clad only in his jeans that were unfastened and shoved part of the way down his hips. Good golly, he was a sexy man. Bad boy, but deep down a good man. A confident man. She thought he was going to help her unzip her shirt, but nope. *Riiiiiiiiiiiip!*

She didn't even care that it was one of her favorite dress-up shirts. This was hot. He yanked the tattered fabric from her arms and eased her back onto the bed with his lips pressed on hers. He tasted so good. So familiar already. Each stroke of his tongue had her wanting him more and more. His hands were everywhere. Not rough, but not gentle. He was exploring her body as he kissed her. Memorizing it, perhaps, and she understood. She was dragging her palms down his chest, across his taut nipples, down the hard mounds of his abs. She hooked her fingers in the band of his briefs and touched the swollen head of his cock. She smiled against his kiss at the soft, appreciative moan that rumbled from his chest.

He was annihilating the friend-zone he'd planned on keeping them in one kiss at a time. Ramsey pulled her ripped-up black jeans down her legs then yanked off her sandals and tossed them behind him so hard they banked off the wall with twin thuds. Her panties came off next, and then her bra, and she should feel so exposed right now as he kissed his way down her stomach with sexy smacking sounds. But she didn't. She was just...getting lost in the moment and, God, what a relief to escape the mess that was always in her head. All those little insecure voices quieted to nothing as Ram kissed down, down, and pushed her legs farther apart as he settled at the edge of the bed, face right there between her thighs. He used his teeth gently as he nipped his way around her sex, teasing, torturing. Vina was writhing toward him by the time he kissed her clit. He slid his tongue along her entrance, and she whispered his name in a plea for more. Lick, lick, lick…he was setting a perfect pace as she moved with him. Sliding her hands into his hair, she spread her knees even wider, rolling her hips as he built the pressure in her middle lick by sexy lick. He'd wrapped his arms around her thighs, and his fingertips were digging into her skin as he pulled her closer with each movement of his jaw. "Ramsey, Ramsey," she whispered, throwing her head back, arching her spine, seeing stars, all of it. He plunged his tongue deep into her, and she was done. She cried out as her body pulsed around him, but he didn't stop. He licked her on and on, pushing the throbbing to last longer as she gasped and twitched.

And then it was Ram's turn. He crawled over her, straddled her, and pushed her up on the mattress, up, up, until her head rested against the headboard. Then he rolled her onto her side, shoved her knees to her chin, and braced himself right at her entrance. She could see him so clearly. This was better than him taking her from behind because she could watch him. Could see his muscles move as he pushed slowly into her. Her orgasm was still pulsing so the pleasure of him inside of her intensified. Ram rolled his eyes closed and let off a soft grunt as he buried himself deep inside her. And then he reared back and slammed into her.

Oh, he was making sure he didn't give into her rules about missionary position. He took care of her first, but he was letting her know he was boss here. Dominant man. He thrust into her harder and faster, his abs flexing as he slid his hand down her arm and then gripped her hip, pinning her in place as he fucked her. And that's what this was. It was fucking. Part of her frowned, but most of her just wanted to get caught up in the moment with him. To see what he was like in the bedroom. Already, she could feel the darkness fading from him. She could breathe easier. God, he was so sexy here, bucking into her smoothly, those pitch-black eyes on her and full of such intensity she couldn't look away if she tried. She was going to finish again. Already, he was building that same pressure. He felt so good inside of her, and timidly, Vina touched her clit.

"Fuck yes," he gritted out. "Keep doing that. I want to watch."

So as he pummeled her from the side, her head banging gently against the headboard, their bodies moving together, she touched between her legs. She could feel him sliding in and out of her, and it was the hottest moment she'd ever been a part of. For the rest of her life, she would never forget the sight of Ramsey's big, powerful body flexing against her. He gripped onto the top of the headboard, and whispered, "Fuck, Vina," as he sped up. "Tell me who you belong to."

"I'm gonna come again," she whispered.

"Tell me," he snarled.

"No one," she said.

Fire flashed in his eyes. Oh, she got it. She wanted him to belong to her too, but he'd already bonded, and giving herself completely to a man who she could never fully possess was terrifying.

Ramsey pulled out of her, rolled her onto her back, and pulled her hand away from her clit. He slid into her slowly and kissed her neck, up, up, until he reached her lips.

This wasn't fucking anymore. It was slow touches, kissing, and a languid pace that said he wasn't in a rush to finish. It was him taking care of her body.

His fingers trailed fire down her skin, and his kisses were gentle. He sipped at her lips like he was tasting her, and as minutes drew on, he became more and more gentle. He stroked her face, traced her jawline as he eased her closer and closer to release. And she did the same for him. She kissed and sucked on his skin, ran her knuckles up his whiskers into his hair. When he locked eyes with her, they weren't black. They were blue, and he looked in awe. He caught her hand and kissed her palm, kissed her wrist, bit it gently, and murmured against the sensitive skin there, "You won't say it yet, but you know you're mine."

He laid his weight over her like a comfortable blanket and pushed deep inside her, stayed deep, made shallow thrusts right there against her clit, and Vina was completely lost in this man. Nothing in her life had ever been like this. Not as significant. Not as important. Something big was happening between her and Ram. Something she didn't understand, but that filled her with hope.

"Ramsey," she whispered as the first pulse of her orgasm shattered her, "I'm yours."

Ram groaned and pushed into her hard, his dick throbbing warmth into her. He gripped the back of her neck and buried his face against her shoulder as he pushed in again and again, filling her with his own release. And when they were done, both spent, he rolled off her, but brought her with him, and he hugged her up tight against his drumming heartbeat.

They didn't say anything for a long time. There was no sound but the soft drone of the air conditioner. Ram had the capacity to do great damage. The knife sunk deep into the wall and the trail of blood downstairs said as much. But with her, he'd gone gentle with a touch. He'd gone tender and caring. Loving.

"I've never done that before," he rumbled at last.

"Done what?"

"Been with a girl slow. Paid attention when I was with her. Fell…"

"What do you mean, fell?"

Ram swallowed audibly. "I can feel your heartbeat against my chest."

Vina pressed her lips to his throat and smiled against his skin . "Me, too." She pressed her palm over his left peck just to feel the slow thrumming there.

"I once heard someone say 'the beating of your heart matters more than the beating of mine.' I can't get it out of my head. I think that's what love is supposed to be like."

Stunned, Vina pressed her lips right over his heartbeat. She knew exactly what he meant. "Someday, say it back to me, okay?"

"Say what?" he asked.

"Say you're mine, too."

He didn't say anything, only stroked his fingertips up and down her spine slowly, as if comforting her was the only thing he could give.

He couldn't give her words or promises yet, but someday, she hoped he would. She hoped she became important enough. That she became big enough, like he was with her.

She hoped that someday he would catch up with her. Until then, she had to be patient because Ramsey was full of damage. And though his damage was beautiful to her, for him it was painful, and he had to heal his heart before he could give it to her.

The beating of your heart matters more than the beating of mine.

Vina sighed and pressed her hand harder over the *bum-bum, bum-bum* of his.

Yeah, that sounded right.

FOURTEEN

The crow sat on the open windowsill, staring out at the full moon. The creature was almost as wide as the window, even with its wings tucked close to his side.

The glossy feathers had a blue sheen to them in the moonlight. Ram stared at her without blinking, just like the first night he'd come to her home.

She'd slept so soundly but woken up to an empty bed. Vina propped the pillow under her cheek and murmured, "Ramsey? Are you okay?"

He didn't move, didn't blink, didn't caw.

He was leaving. The realization hurt in ways she'd never been hurt before. Ramsey had slept with her and bonded to her, but his crow had not. And now that he was Changed, he would hurt them forever by going to Ten.

"Stay with me," she pleaded, her eyes prickling with tears. *Pick me.*

Three breaths, and Ramsey turned away from her, bunched his body, and then disappeared into the night.

The crow was punishing the man.

She wasn't the type of girl to stick around while a man pined for another. At some point, she had to be enough or it would destroy her, just like Ethan had talked about.

Five minutes was all she dared to wait in his bed before she got up, tears burning her eyes, and dressed in her jeans and one of Ramsey's T-shirts since her blouse was in shreds.

The walk of shame was awful. It was worse because she'd thought sleeping with Ram was bigger than it actually was. She'd been tricked. God, she was a fool.

Sniffing, she closed Ramsey's door behind her and made her way downstairs. It was three in the morning, and no one was here except the one person she wished wasn't.

Ethan was playing pool by himself with a half-empty bottle of Maker's Mark near one of the corner pockets. He didn't look at her as she made her way past. Just lined up for another shot and said, "I told you."

She hated him. "Bye, Ethan," she choked out. The bonus to Ramsey's crow shitting on their relationship and choosing another was she wouldn't have to see Ethan ever again.

"Here," he said. She turned just in time to catch a set of keys. "There is a truck parked on the side of the building. I'll have someone pick it up tomorrow. Don't fuck it up."

She lifted the keys. "Thanks, I guess."

He didn't answer, just gave her his back, and went back to shooting pool.

When the door swung closed behind her, she splayed her legs outside, looked up at the moon, and huffed a sigh.

How could one day be the best and worst of her life?

The truck was an old black F150, but there was someone leaning against the driver's side door. It was the woman from earlier with the dark hair and blond streaks. The one who had told the girls to leave.

"You were supposed to come sooner," she said.

"What?" Vina asked, shaking her head in confusion.

"I mean, you were supposed to get to his crow before Tenlee did. You were late." She sighed and looked Vina up and down with a slight frown to her dark eyebrows. "You're not what I expected."

"I'm not what anyone expects."

"Good." The woman pushed off the side of the truck. "I gave my heart to a man once who couldn't give me his in return. I did it out of duty, so I understand the sacrifice. Sometimes it'll hurt, but that hurt will make you stronger and stronger until nothing can break you. It won't feel like it at first, but you're a lucky one."

"I don't understand," Vina murmured.

The woman walked away but over her shoulder she said, "Be patient with him."

"I'm Vina!" she called.

"The boys call me Momma Crow." And then she disappeared around the back corner of the building.

Okay. Well, that was a weird ending to an already weird night. Be patient with him? With Ramsey? No spank you. She wasn't chasing some man who wouldn't choose her back. He'd slept with her and then left to stalk Ten. Another wave of pain washed through her.

She was used to driving bigger vehicles, so she got home just fine in the giant truck. She couldn't stop imagining Ram in a tree on Two Claws property, watching Ten's house where she slept. His focus was on her, while Vina's heart felt like it was breaking in two.

Stupid *hope.*

Everyone spoke that word like it was a good thing, but it wasn't. Hope was a bomb disguised as a butterfly, sitting inside a heart, waiting for a misstep that would set it off.

And the worst part, the very worst part, was that no one expected a butterfly to be lethal. To have the potential to change a person from the inside out, disintegrate layer after layer of their souls until there was nothing recognizable left.

This was her second time to give hope a chance. She felt so stupid.

But...she'd been through rejection before, and she knew her limits. She would survive. She would spend a week of nights lying on the shower floor with miniature plastic bottles of wine, crying until her tears ran dry. And then after a while, it would hurt less. Or she would get used to the pain. Or both.

Maybe she was just one of those people destined to be alone. Maybe that was her fate. Maybe rejection was toughening her up to endure a lonely life.

Feeling utterly broken, she pulled onto her street, the truck's headlights making a wide arch to her duplex. Something strange reflected from the tree branches in front that made Vina lurch to a stop. She wiped her eyes and blinked hard, thinking she was imagining the large crow sitting on the bottom branch of the tree.

"R-Ramsey?" she murmured over the soft sound of the heavy metal playing in the truck.

She crept forward, parked in the driveway, killed the engine, and got out.

The white diamond on the crow's chest was unmistakable. It was Ram.

"You didn't go to Ten," she said to the frozen crow.

He turned his head and looked at her with his other unblinking eye.

"Tonight, you didn't choose her."

The crow spread its wings and flew down to the yard where her plastic chair and cooler still sat.

"Okay then," she murmured, utterly stunned.

She made her way through the dirt and weeds and sat down gingerly in the lawn chair. Ramsey didn't back away from her or tense up. He just looked up at the moon.

Ramsey was two beings. A crow and a man. Just like she was a woman and a moose. But for him, the man and the animal were completely separate. Two different personalities, two different creatures altogether.

And she had to win them both.

And tonight, the King of Crows had chosen a moon-gazing date with her.

Vina smiled as potent relief washed over her. There was no rejection. He was giving them a chance.

And there was the butterfly…bomb…butterfly…bomb…in her chest once again. There was that hope.

FIFTEEN

The Crow watched her. Vina. Pretty name. Pretty girl. He could see why Ramsey's heart beat fast around her. But he'd already picked…right? He was only supposed to pick one time. It was ingrained in him. One chance. One choice, and he'd picked The Origin. The first squirrel shifter. Tenlee. Tenleeeeeeee. She'd been special, but she didn't look at him like Vina did.

This was confusing.

Vina Fiona Marsh. Ramsey had read her folder. The Crow had read it with him. Ram didn't realize how present The Crow was all the time. He was the real king. The real Alpha. Ram didn't exist right now because The Crow didn't want him to.

This moment, he wanted to himself. He'd been there when Ramsey had slept with this woman, this shifter, earlier tonight. And he'd felt something strange happening to his human half. It was light. It was an easy moment and one that didn't belong to creatures of the dark like him.

Ramsey, for a second, had been happy. Content. At peace.

This girl was the reason.

So The Crow had taken Ram's body, determined to fly to Tenlee and remind Ram of who they'd chosen. To remind him about loyalty, but on the flight, The Crow thought of something that changed everything.

He and Ram hadn't chosen Ten.

Only he had. Ram was just along for the ride. Oh, he had felt every ounce of rejection right along with Ram. Every dodged kiss. Every time she pulled away. Every time she avoided holding his hand, or even looking at him. She'd stayed a squirrel just so she didn't have to talk to him. And Ram...Ram had been demolished slowly because of The Crow's choice.

The one moment of happiness that Ram had in bed with this girl? It had changed everything.

Maybe a creature of darkness could have both. Shadow and light. Ram would be the shadow and maybe this Vina-girl...maybe she could be the light.

He watched her fold her long legs as she sat in the plastic chair in the middle of the yard. She was wearing one of Ram's Harley Davidson T-shirts. He smiled to himself as he remembered Ram ripping her fancy shirt off her. Their bodies did good together. They liked each other.

He was supposed to remind Ram about being loyal to Tenlee, but he was curious again. He'd watched her before, but he couldn't figure her out. Dominant and submissive, soft yet tough. He wanted to know everything about her. Sometimes he let Ram be present just a little when he came to see Vina, but not tonight. Tonight, this date with her belonged to him.

He sat on the ground beside her, head cocked, and looked up at her, waiting.

"When I was a kid, I didn't like being different. It took me a long time to get used to being a shifter. I was mad at my dad for making me one. Only boys are supposed to be born shifters, and there I was, a girl. A moose. So rare, we couldn't even find a Clan. It was just us. I didn't have much control over my temper when I was a kid, so I was homeschooled through elementary. I was lonely, and that only made me angrier. My parents could see me getting more and more closed off, so one night, when I was ten, my dad took me out into the woods. My mom was human, and she came along, but she stopped at the edge of the trees, set out a blanket, and started reading a book. She had a picnic basket packed, but she wouldn't let me eat anything.

"Before that, Changes were a private thing. Me and my dad Changed at different times in the woods right behind our house. I hardly saw his moose. But that night, he told me to Change behind some brush, and when I got up, all shaky on my long legs, body aching from Turning, he was waiting there. And Ram...he was massive. You'll see my animal someday, and it will change the way you look at me, but my dad? He's a titan. Massive antlers that two kids could sit on easily. Ten feet tall at the shoulders. Hooves the size of my face." She put her flattened palm in front of her face to show him how big. "He stood so proudly there in the woods, his thick neck holding those antlers high. I remember thinking he looked like some prehistoric mammal, just huge. He was three times my size. And that night, he took me all around the woods. Didn't get frustrated when I was jumping and running around his legs, tripping him up. His moose is the patient type. Slow-moving. Easy-going. Until…" Vina licked her lips and swallowed hard. "I could smell the bear, and it scared me. Dad's nostrils were twitching so I could tell he could smell him too, but he kept walking down the trail, right toward the scent. I kept hanging back. I wanted to go to my mom where it was safe. It wasn't fun being in the woods anymore. We were being hunted. I was small. I was the target. Dad was moving so slow, his head swaying from side to side like his enormous body was sore just walking. He wouldn't be able to outrun a brown bear."

Vina stretched her legs out and wrapped her arms around her middle. Her eyes had this faraway look, and The Crow had a strange urge to scoot closer to her. So he did.

"When the attack came, it hurt. I could hear that animal crashing through the brush, and it was so loud. I ran, but he was on me in seconds. His claws raked right down my back, and the weight of the grizzle buckled my legs. I went down like a sack of rocks. I thought I was dying, it hurt so bad, and then I saw him. My dad. He wasn't slow anymore. He was as fast as a snake bite. He charged and pushed that bear right off me with his massive antlers. I laid there shocked as I watched him stomp the life out of that predator. I realized in that moment that the bear hadn't been hunting us at all. My dad had been hunting it. He was showing me what I would be capable of. He was giving me pride in my animal. He was showing me I could protect myself. No fear in his eyes as he killed the thing that had raked its claws against my back. And then he came back over to me, cleaned the blood off my ribs, and then we walked back to my mom.

"She was crying, but smiling, and I didn't understand. Later she told me how hard it was for my dad growing up with no moose to show him how to be. He was adopted by boar shifters and had always felt out of place and alone. And she was happy he was figuring out how to be there for me while I learned how to control my animal. We told her about the bear, and then she let us eat from the picnic basket, all breakfast food because we'd been out in the woods all night. And from then on, it was tradition. My mom would pull an all-nighter, waiting for me and my dad to come back from the woods. Always waiting with breakfast. That chip on my shoulder disappeared little by little until I was proud of the animal, proud of being different. And someday, when I have sons, it doesn't matter what animal they are born with. I'll be there for them like my parents were for me. I'm going to teach them to be proud of their animals."

The Crow stared at the beautiful girl. She wasn't just pretty anymore; she was a beauty. Moonlight hitting her high cheekbones, hair wild from sex, Harley T-shirt resting on her full breasts, eyes rimmed with the gold of her animal's.

She reached over and brushed her fingertips down his back. Voluntarily, she touched him, and it felt so good. Vina's smile was easy. It was just for him. She'd shared a part of herself and then looked at him like nothing else mattered.

And her willing touch...

Okay, Ram.

Okay.

SIXTEEN

Did she like coffee? Pastries? Waffles? God, he didn't know how to do this. Ramsey didn't do sensitive shit. He'd tried with Tenlee for about fourteen seconds before she shut that down, but Vina was out of his league, and she deserved a good man.

He was going to get everything and just hope for the best. Ramsey gave the to-go server at the Partridge Pancake House in town his giant order, and then watched, not-so-patiently, through the window to the kitchen the cook work on their food.

The to-go server looked uncomfortable at his hovering near the counter, so with a huffed breath, Ramsey sank down in the waiting area and stretched out his leg, his riding boot making a clump sound on the red brick flooring. The Crow had let him in last night. Well, after Vina was sleepy and talking in circles to him in her front yard. She'd started nodding off, so he'd Changed back and carried her to bed. She'd wrapped her arms around his neck, rested her cheek against his chest and, for a while, he'd sat on the edge of her mattress just holding her.

She was changing everything.

"Are you one of those animal men?" a woman with perfect blond curls and a high-necked baby blue sundress asked from beside him. She clutched her matching blue purse in her lap. "One of those shifters?"

Ramsey frowned at her and turned away in his chair.

"'Cause your eyes are black and evil-looking."

"I'm not evil," he gritted out. *Settle down, she's just a nosy woman, probably doesn't mean any harm.*

She tapped him on the shoulder, and he barely avoided the snarl that bubbled up his throat. "Here's the card for my church. We could get that demon out of you and give you a normal life."

Shocked, Ramsey stared at the card in her hand. "Seriously?" he asked, turning toward her. "You'd exorcise my animal so I can be like you?"

"Well, yes." She arched her perfectly manicured brows and wiggled the card impatiently.

For a moment, Ramsey considered walking away and waiting for Vina's breakfast outside, but fuck this. He yanked the card from her fingertips and offered her an empty smile. Then he ripped it slowly into little pieces and murmured, "I like my demon where he is. Why don't you go worry about your own life?"

"Ramsey," said the girl behind the checkout counter, pushing a trio of plastic bags of food toward him.

"Oh, I'm not worried about mine," the blonde said, shaking her head slowly. "I know exactly where I'm going."

Ramsey huffed a laugh. "Same. You have a good and judgmental day, ya hear?" He stood and made his way to check out, paid, yanked the food off the counter, and made his way past the blonde and outside.

Demon. She wasn't that far off. His crow was capable of horrible things, but so was the man side of him. That lady was a pill. Was that what the public thought of shifters? He hadn't really paid attention to the news lately. He'd had other shit to worry about.

It was barely dawn outside, six in the morning, and cloudy. He loved cloudy days and didn't care at all what that said about him. He bet Vina loved the sun. She was sunny spring days and he was overcast winter, and the demon in him cawed happily because he loved that contrast. She was different. She was what he needed.

And that made him want to take care of her. To make her want to stick around.

Ramsey, I'm yours—the three most life-altering words to a broken crow like him. And he was going to spend the remainder of his sanity making her feel special like she deserved.

The drive to Vina's house was a short one. She lived right in town, just a few streets away from the pancake place. He cut the engine to his Harley, settled it on the kickstand, and made his way to her door. "What?" he asked the woman glaring at him, standing on the front porch of the duplex next door in a robe and fuzzy bunny slippers.

"You are the most inconsiderate people on the whole planet. It's six in the morning and you are blaring that monstrous bike all around town. Perfect match for her." She jammed a finger at Vina's front door.

Ramsey chuckled. "Thank you. I like her, too." He offered the battle-ax a wink and let himself in Vina's front door, which was unlocked. He was gonna have to have a serious talk to her about locking up. He'd locked it when he left this morning, but she must've checked the mail or messed with the trash bins or something.

He could hear her singing over the running spray of the shower and grinned to himself. "Smells Like Teen Spirit." Atta girl. She was so unique. So cute. So many layers that he wanted to know about.

"Babe!" he called, giving her the warning that he was back. Babe?

The metal clasps on the shower curtain screeched across the bar. "Ramsey? Did you just call me 'babe'?"

He laughed. "Apparently, that's where we are in this relationship now."

"Friends who have naked parties and call each other babe?" she asked. Her voice was infused with excitement.

Ramsey opened the bathroom door.

Vina screeched and yanked the curtain over to

cover herself. "I didn't know you were coming in! I just washed off my make-up!"

He laughed, pulling the curtain back again. "You look like a disheveled raccoon."

Vina tried to cover herself again, but he wouldn't allow it. "Let me see you in all your naked, wet, make-up streaming down your face, glory and get it done with."

"I want you to be attracted to me," she wailed, covering her face with her dripping hands.

He was laughing in earnest now, trying to pry her hands off her face with one hand and holding onto her breakfast with the other. "Woman, I already saw you. You're the cutest fuckin' raccoon I've ever encountered, and I would still fuck you right here in the shower, runny make-up and all."

"You would?" she squeaked.

"Yes! Look at you! Curves for days, them long stems, naked, dripping wet... I ain't even lookin' at your make-up!"

She pulled her hands away and pouted out her bottom lip. God, she was so cute and sexy. How could a woman master both at the same time?

"Feel," he murmured, drawing her hand to the fly

of his pants so she could feel his boner. "That's all you."

Her pout turned to a smile, and she squeezed right over his balls. God, he really did want to fuck her now. "How much time do you have before work?"

"I have to leave in forty-five minutes."

"I brought you breakfast...." He rolled his eyes closed at how good her kneading little fingers felt. "Damn woman. I was gonna try to keep off you this morning, but fuck it. Come here."

When he pulled her from the shower, she did something that shocked him and went right down onto the bright purple bath rug on her hands and knees. Then she arched her spine and presented her cute little ass for him and, holy fuck, she was the sexiest woman alive. Soccer Mom wasn't home right now, just Sexy-AF-Vixen.

Ramsey couldn't think of anything else but the curve of that ass. Like a rutting animal, he dropped to his knees and unfastened his jeans as fast as he could. She was soaking wet when he slid into her and, God, the pressure felt so good on his dick. Fast and hard. That's all he had to offer right now. He reached around and pressed his fingers to her clit as he bucked into her. Fuck, every time he was balls deep inside her, it was ecstasy. His perfect girl. So wet and tight. She was moving with him, gasping like she was close and, thank God, because he was there. "Fuck, Vina," he gritted out as he rammed into her and came, his dick throbbing hard. And then she was pulsing too, panting his name—so fucking beautiful.

He huffed a breath and leaned onto her back, kissed her wet hair, and brushed his fingertips up and down her ribs to her full breasts and back. He didn't want to get off her, didn't want that disconnect, but she had to get ready, and he wanted her to have time to eat before she left for work.

He nipped at the back of her neck and growled, "I like fucking you right out of the shower. Clean girl, and I get to make you dirty again."

She gave a soft giggle that made his stomach clench with something easy. Something that felt good. Happiness? Damn, what was that?

He slid out of her and sat back on his bent knees, unable to take his eyes from his cum dripping down her inner thighs. He fucking loved it. His. She was his. He wanted her full of him all the time. A possessiveness took over him as he smiled with pride. She rocked back on her knees and leaned her back against his chest. He held her there, arms around her, lips pressed to her neck as he smiled and smiled. Couldn't stop smiling. God, what was wrong with him? Vina was breaking him in a good way.

Against her ear, he murmured, "I'm gonna get your breakfast ready. And you're gonna get all gussied up in your fancy work clothes and look like a proper lady, but all day, you'll think about how you got fucked on the bathroom floor by your man, and deep down, you'll know you're a badass for me. I'm gonna go handle some stuff with the Clan, and tonight, I'm gonna take you out. We'll be perfectly proper in public, and then I'm gonna bring you home and remind you of what a bad girl you really are."

He swatted her ass and reveled in the happy sound she made as she rocked her head back against him. That woman had the best reactions to his touch.

He kissed her neck, nipped her, kissed her ear, nipped her, then gripped her hair and angled her face gently to taste her lips. Then he stood slowly, careful not to let her fall back, and left her there on the bathroom floor, looking like she had no idea what he'd just done to her body.

"I like you," she whispered in a dreamy voice right as he was leaving.

Good girl. My girl.

And then he leaned against the doorframe and threw all his rules away with an admission he'd sworn to never give another girl as long as he lived. "I like you back."

And if the slow, happy smile on her lips was anything to go by, she knew exactly what he really meant.

SEVENTEEN

Date niiiiiight!

Today had been crazy-busy because of the rain. Usually, youth baseball practices were held at the fields right behind the community center, but it had started pouring around noon. The fields got too muddy, so the coaches had to bring the practices into the two gyms they had on either side of the building. Add that to the support group meetings, karate lessons, sculpture class and baking class, and Vina had been rushing around trying to make sure everything was running smoothly and that none of the teachers, coaches, or students needed anything. And she'd had to work late. It was seven before she said her goodbyes to the senior coordinator.

Bright side, though, Mrs. Villanueva had invited her to stay for the cooking class, and so Vina had spent her extremely late lunch break making cupcakes with a group of rowdy but fun teenagers in the afterschool program. The cupcakes were chocolate with chocolate frosting and chocolate sprinkles. Crow cupcakes for the guys.

And right as she was packing them in her car to leave, she got a text from Ramsey.

Hey pretty girl, I have a meeting until a little later. I'll call you as soon as I'm out.

Hardworkin' man. She only had a guess how much work he did to run a Clan as big as Red Dead Mayhem. Or the effort it had taken him to become Alpha. Nope, she didn't want to think about whatever illegal ways his Clan made money because she was high on happiness right now, and nothing could dampen her mood. Not today.

She really needed to Change. Okay, new plan. She would drop the cupcakes off at the clubhouse so the guys would have a snack after they got done with their meeting, and then she would go to the woods near Corvallis and Change and do moose stuff until Ramsey was freed up to do date night and ravage her body. Because that was definitely happening. Her mind had been in the gutter all day since he'd taken her on the shower rug this morning. That man was hot as sin and twice as naughty.

Already she felt like a secret bad girl just being around him. He made her want to make questionable decisions, ride motorcycles, wear revealing clothes, and learn to play pool better. And...and...live! She wanted to *live*. She wanted to break from the normal routine of work, eat, sleep, repeat and have adventures.

Ram liked her. He told her as much this morning, and then he'd watched her eat the giant breakfast he'd brought. And he didn't even look disgusted when she had syrup on her face. He'd just smiled and kissed it off, and that was special. She bet the next time he brought her food, it would be double the waffles and no pastries. He seemed to genuinely enjoy taking care of her and paid attention. How sweet that a busy, rough-and-tumble outlaw like him could have the capacity to think about her so thoroughly.

She was falling so hard for him that she had moments of fear as she imagined her life when he got bored with her. That's what could happen for shifters who couldn't bond. They could just end up friends. But she couldn't let her past and the rejection of her lost marriage hurt what she and Ramsey were exploring. What they were building. She wouldn't make him pay for the hurt she'd gone through since he wasn't making her pay for his pain.

The parking lot to the crow's clubhouse was completely full, and the entire street out front was crowded with news vans. Vina slowed and frowned at a woman in a business suit holding a microphone, talking into a camera some man was holding.

What the heck?

She coasted past them, and when she couldn't find a spot in the parking lot, she parked her Explorer along the curb near the row of Harleys out front. There was a crowd outside, but the only person she recognized was Momma Crow, who stood at the front door turning reporters away. She looked pissed, jamming her finger at the street, veins popping in her neck, yelling something Vina couldn't hear from here.

As she got the cupcakes out of the front seat, a man in a starched blue suit and navy tie held a microphone to his lips as he crowded her and asked, "Are you with the crow shifters?"

She ignored him as she balanced the cardboard box of pastries in front of her and kicked her door closed.

The man stood right in front of her, blocking her path to the door. "Are you acquainted with Ramsey Hunt. Are you pledged to the Alpha?"

"No comment. Get out of my way," she gritted through a stiff jaw.

"Are you aware of the long history of violence with shifters?"

"Move." She dodged to the right, but he moved with her, standing between her and the door.

"Are you one of the accused—"

"Get the fuck out of my way before I stomp you to oblivion. I said no comment!"

And then Momma Crow was there. "Back off her! She isn't a part of this. She is just making a delivery, you prick. That's how you treat a lady? Look in her arms. She's clearly here delivering snacks for a private club meeting." Momma Crow gripped her elbow and led her past the man.

"Did you get that?" the reporter murmured to his camera man behind them. "She's definitely one of them. Did you see her eyes?"

Crap. "What's going on?" she whispered as Momma Crow led her inside.

As soon as she shut the door to the clubhouse, the woman turned on her. "Who did you tell about this place?"

Vina felt slapped. "No one. I haven't even told my parents I've been matched to Ramsey yet."

"Friends?"

"I don't have any here. I tried, but I don't really fit in. I swear I've told no one."

"What are these, Vina?" She pulled four little black contraptions no bigger than marbles from her jeans pocket.

Vina stared at them, shaking her head. She wasn't good at guessing games. "Anal beads?"

"Oh, my God. The worst part is I can tell you are actually confused by these. Vina, these are bugs. We found one in Ramsey's room, one in the meeting room, one under the pool table, and one under the lip of the bar. This place was clean before you showed up."

"Wait...you think I planted bugs in here? Where would I even get those? I don't even like spy movies!"

"I don't know, but it's really awful timing, Vina,"

Momma Crow said low. "We have a shit-storm of reporters outside, bugs in the house, and the only thing different around here is you. The boys are all up in arms—"

There was yelling behind the big double doors to the meeting room. "Either she fucking goes or we do! I'm not staying in a clubhouse with a snitch. She's dangerous, Ramsey! You get that, right?" Was that Ethan's voice? "She puts your Clan at risk, and we were already in the middle of an Armageddon. Your desperation to fix yourself is putting us right in the public's eye. We are going to take direct hits. You get that, right?"

"Sit the fuck down!" Ramsey bellowed. Something slammed against a table.

"That's because of me?" Vina asked, panicked.

"Yeah." Momma Crow shook her head slowly, her eyes pooled with worry. "Even if you didn't do this, there was a storm building before you came. Ram is strong, girl. He's so strong. But he's been limping, and his Clan has seen his weakness for too long. And now he's picked another girl who they see as a risk, and it puts his place as Alpha in jeopardy. They're tired. Tired and desperate for things to get easier. You understand?"

Vina stared at the door. Three or four men were yelling now, and she couldn't even make out what they were saying. There was a roaring in her ears.

"But...I just wanted to help him. I wanted to make him okay. For him to be happy." Tears prickled in her eyes. "He just said he had a meeting, and that he would call me after. We were supposed to go out tonight. I wanted..." Vina swallowed hard. "I wanted someone I could hang out with after work. I wanted Ramsey." She looked at Momma Crow with wide eyes. "Am I...am I ruining his life?"

There was a banging on the front door, and even through the frosted glass, she could see the crowd of reporters. Why now? Shifters had been exposed months ago. It had been a slow leak, and now it was a tornado? A tornado focused on Red Dead Mayhem? It didn't make any sense.

Her phone dinged with a text message. And another. And another. Wiping her eyes on the shoulder of her blouse, she set the cupcakes on the pool table and pulled her bejeweled phone from her purse. It was her dad.

You're on the news.

Your mom and I just saw you on the news.

What's happening?

Do we call you?

You never pick up.

You cussed on TV.

You never cuss.

Are you okay?

Oh, geez. "That snippet of me already made it to the news," she told Momma Crow, who immediately jogged to the big flat screen television behind the bar and started poking buttons on the remote. "My parents are worried."

"Well, honey, they probably should be," Momma Crow murmured. "Look."

On the TV was a shot of the outside of the clubhouse, apparently live, and the reporter, a saucy brunette, was talking about how there appeared to be some kind of disturbance inside. They were filming the shadows against the meeting room windows, and on TV, it looked like the boys were damn near close to fighting. At least six of them had Changed to crows and were dive-bombing. The sound of shattering glass was deafening. The banging on the front door was getting louder, Vina's phone was going off too fast for her to even respond to texts, and every news channel Momma Crow flipped to was breaking news of the boys' rap sheets, talking about how shifters were a menace to society. And yep, on channel four, there was Vina, cussing at the reporter with a dozen chocolate cupcakes clutched to her boobs.

"What do I do?" Vina asked.

Jamming a finger at Vina, Momma Crow ordered, "You go up to Ramsey's room and don't come down. Stay there, and don't come down here no matter what you hear. The shit is hitting the fan, girl." She jogged to the door of the meeting room, her black stiletto heels clacking against the wood with ever hurried step.

The animal inside of her was getting bigger. She was burning through Vina's veins at the thought of Ramsey in the middle of that fight, being filmed without his permission as he defended her. It wasn't fair. She didn't do anything wrong, and he was going to get hurt because of her. He was going to lose his Clan, or worse.

When Mother Crow threw open the door, the bellowing of men's voices was so loud the confusing words clanged around in her head.

She could see him. Ramsey. Her Ramsey. He was throwing a punch, his face all cut up by talons, fending off a crowd of his own people as they backed him to the wall.

She had her orders from Momma Crow, but for the life of her, Vina couldn't take a single step toward the stairs.

The moose in her was no coward. She was a protector, a defender, and her person was bleeding.

Momma Crow was screaming for them to bring the fight into the bar, but the boys weren't listening. They were too full of bloodlust, lunging, punching, beating each other. Rike was fighting Kasey, and Ethan was throwing his knuckles at Ramsey, who turned and slammed his Second against the wall and returned the pummeling. Crows dove for them, but if Ramsey felt their talons slicing at the back of his neck and shoulders, he showed no sign of pain. Just relentless, merciless fighting.

They would kill each other, those men in there. Those outlaws. Those bikers who were supposed to be bound by allegiance to the King of Crows but had somehow become so broken that their Clan was imploding.

The windows were broken, and she could see the flash of cameras. This was very bad. And it was about to get so much worse because, as the Clan surged toward Ramsey, intent on de-throning their Alpha, Vina doubled over the pain in her middle.

She always felt sick right before a Change and hit the floor on hands and knees. She dry-heaved and then cried out a warning. "Stop!" If they didn't back off him, she couldn't control what her animal would do to them.

Dad had taught her to be a hunter, to protect the people she loved, and she loved Ramsey. Loved him. Loved. Him.

His entire Clan needed to back away, or she would paint the floors with their gore.

She screamed in agony as she fought the animal, but it was no use. Never had been. She never did win against a full-grown, aggressive female moose.

That animal ripped out of her cell by cell until her human skin was nothing and her tough, furred hide created her new shape, her eight-foot-tall shape because Dad had passed some gnarly genetics to his only child. He'd made a monster moose just like himself. And sure, she didn't have his antlers, but she was every bit as powerful, and all these crows hurting her mate were so utterly and uncompromisingly fucked.

She bellowed out her death chant. She roared like a bear when she was pissed, but they should understand what was coming for them. Vina charged the room, her hooves slamming against the wooden floors so hard, they cracked into halves. She was destruction, never meant to Change in a building. That saying "like a bull in a china shop?" That was accurate.

She slammed into the half-closed door and lowered her head and took the crowd with her. Four men were pinned against the opposite wall by the window within moments, and the table where they held their meetings? She barreled right through it to get to another three crows. With a crash, the table was nothing but splinters.

She charged and thrashed her hooves at anything that moved. Her fury was infinite. The boys were yelling now, bleeding. Broken. They were panicking and Changing. Crows were everywhere. Broken glass shone like diamonds across the floor. It looked like it was raining black feathers. Talons sliced at her hide, but she didn't care. It would take a hundred crows to bleed her out. Six were left, eyes full of murder and trained on Ramsey. He was straddling Ethan, fist blasting across his jaw over and over. His eyes were pitch black and promised death, and as much as Vina wanted to allow it, she couldn't in front of the cameras. They would use him as an example and lock him away, so she did the only thing she could. She reared up and lashed out with her hooves at the men beating on Ramsey from behind, and then she swung the top of her head against Ramsey hard enough to knock him back into the wall with a *bang!*

Ramsey was on the kill though, and his eyes hadn't left Ethan, even when he hit the wall. It was an Alpha challenge, and she'd interrupted. The flashing camera lights were so bright, so irritating to her eyes, she shook her head, her floppy ears slapping at the sides of her face. Momma Crow was pressed up against the wall beside Rike, clutching her chest as she stared at Vina in horror. Her moose had that effect on people.

Ethan and the others were writhing and groaning on the floor in pain, and the crows that had Changed had flown out the broken windows and into the night.

Click, click, click went the cameras. She hated them. Vina looked over her shoulder and bellowed again. She wished she could trample them all.

When she looked back at Ramsey, he'd jerked his focus off Ethan, and his eyes were now locked on her. Black eyes. Shocked eyes. His chest heaved with his ragged breath, and the *drip, drip, drip* of the blood pitter-pattered onto the floor. It was the only sound other than the clicking of cameras.

I'm sorry. She wished she could talk and say those words out loud. *I'm so sorry.*

Ramsey looked from her to the flashing cameras that lit up his face then back to Ethan.

"Everyone who remains, get into the bar," he demanded in a hoarse yet powerful voice.

A dozen broken men reacted in an instant. She couldn't even guess how many broken ribs were in this room, but the men dragged their pained bodies to the other room with grunts of agony until only Ramsey and Vina remained.

This was it. This was where he would tell her to leave. To reprimand her for stepping in the middle of an Alpha challenge. This was where he would look at her moose in disgust as he realized what an aggressive, out of control monster she was. This was the moment he would reject her, because how could he not? Every king deserved a queen, and she wasn't that. Not even close.

He straightened to his full height, his gaze steady on her. She closed her eyes, ready for the words that would hurt the most.

And then he spoke. "My name is Ramsey Hunt. This is my mate, Vina Marsh. We will conduct interviews in three days' time at the community center in Darby if you give us space and give us peace enough to clean up our home."

Vina jerked her eyes open. *What?*

Ramsey wasn't looking at her, though. He was addressing the people outside.

"You've caused enough trouble with my people," he gritted out. "This is private property, and you are all trespassing. You got what you came for. Now get the fuck out."

And Vina, the giant moose shifter who'd expected to be rejected, stood there on locked legs, stunned into stillness over what he'd just done.

Ramsey had just told the entire world that she was his mate.

EIGHTEEN

She was beautiful.

Ramsey watched her saunter through the door she'd busted wide open. The second, the very second, he'd taken his focus off Ethan and laid eyes on her, something had changed. Something inside of him had snapped like a taut rubber band.

His crow had really seen her. Graceful. Lethal. Pure power. Protecting him because he could see exactly what she was doing. He'd figured out her intentions the second the bloodlust ebbed. The instant her light touched him, logic had returned. There were cameras, and he'd been intent on that Alpha Challenge Ethan had called. He'd been focused on the kill so no crow in his Clan would ever

Challenge him again.

She'd pushed Ramsey off Ethan in time. She'd saved Ethan. Saved Ramsey in the process because now he wouldn't rot in some jail cell for a murder reporters would have caught on camera.

She'd pulled the traitorous Clan off him and made the fight fair. Protective mate. And that's what she was—his mate.

His crow realized that the instant he set his eyes, heart, and soul on her moose.

Fuck, she was gorgeous. Huge, moving slow as she clomped past him and back through the splintered doorway, but he'd seen her. He would never mistake her for slow. She'd been faster than any punch he'd thrown. She'd broken the fuckin' Clan.

He'd nearly allowed a smile when the Clan dragged their aching bodies out of here.

His lady didn't play around. Sexy Vina.

On a whim, he reached out and brushed his fingers down her ribs as she passed, tracing old silver claw-mark scars there. The story behind them was right at the tip of his memories. Maybe she'd told The Crow what happened to her.

Mine.

Ramsey did allow the smile now.

Mine, The Crow repeated, the word rattling around in his head.

The poisonous dark that had filled him was just…gone. She'd banished it.

Oh, sure, he could still see the ghosts. They were gathered here where so much death had almost happened. They were drawn to the bad energy that clung to the room. But some were nodding, as though he'd done something right.

Something right.

How long had it been since he'd felt like he'd done anything right?

You picked her right, The Crow whispered.

Chills rippled up his arms as he stood there, watching her make her way to the bar, to Momma Crow and Rike.

The Clan was in tatters. What had happened tonight wasn't okay. It wouldn't be okay for a long time. There would have to be big changes in Red Dead Mayhem. And whoever came back, begging to keep their place, their rank, they would have to face the public beside Ram and Vina.

The war with Two Claws was done and gone. His

bond with Tenlee? Ramsey stretched his heart out but could no longer find a trace of the shadows she'd left behind.

Vina had fixed him.

She'd fixed him.

She'd repaired an unredeemable, unsalvageable man. She'd stuck with him, knowing he was bonded to another, and she gave him space and loyalty to figure out what he needed.

He needed Vina. Wanted her. Coveted her. And he was going to spend the rest of his life showing her how important she was, because this woman was a true ride-or-die. And she deserved devotion.

She'd given him hope, and he would repay her by giving her the devotion of a crow.

He felt the cameras on his back as he followed what was left of the Clan into the next room, followed his mate into their future. He knew the worst was behind him, and ahead was a future he could work for, covet, and be happy with.

Vina turned and looked at him with soft brown eyes. Worry pooled there. Worry for him. He didn't know how he'd lucked into her. Big, badass, scarred-up moose, her ears nearly touching the ceiling, and she wasn't taken with bloodlust or anger. Her eyes said a hundred things that he understood in an instant. That The Crow understood.

And the biggest one of those...the most important...were these:

I'll have your back always.

I'm yours.

I love you.

And from her soft, relieved sigh, barely audible above the chaos around them, she'd read the same in his eyes.

NINETEEN

"Can I open my eyes yet?" Vina asked over the rumble of the Harley.

Ram had been riding with one hand, holding hers tight to his stomach with the other. It had been two days since he'd seen her animal, and he'd broken all his own rules. Now, he touched her all the time and made her feel safe and cared for. She loved it.

"One more minute. Almost there," he said.

With a happy smile, Vina rested her cheek against his back. The last two days had been chaos. They'd been hard. Ramsey was in meeting after meeting with the remaining crows, Ethan had disappeared into the night, and Ram thought he was starting a new Clan with the traitors. They'd had to order supplies to repair all the damage she'd done to the clubhouse, and the phone was ringing off the hook with requests for interview spots for tomorrow.

She would be sitting beside her mate in front of the cameras, answering questions about what and who she was in one tiny day. Every time she thought about it, her nerves got the best of her and she felt like Changing.

Tonight, Ramsey had drawn her between his splayed legs as he'd rested against the pool table, kissed her knuckles, and murmured, "You wanna get out of here for a while? Just you and me?"

She was tired from the long day, but it had still been an easy answer. Of course she did.

Tonight was warm wind on her skin, a full moon, and the instruction to close her eyes when Ram had turned off on a dirt road.

The Harley slowed, and she pressed a kiss to his spine just to quell the excitement that bubbled up inside of her. She loved surprises.

Ram cut the engine and gripped her thigh. "Last night, when I was right on the edge of sleep, something really cool happened. The Crow showed me things. Things I'd missed. Things he'd hidden from me. He showed me every moment he'd spent at your house. Even the ones I remember, he gave them to me in detail. As I watched you through these memories, you became more and more beautiful to him. Like this tarnished object that was getting all polished up. And Tenlee, or his memories of her, got dimmer and duller. And then he gave me your story of your parents and the bear, when you got those scars, and I could feel him falling in love with you too, just like I was."

Vina's breath hitched as she lost it, and she gripped his middle closer. "You're falling in love with me?"

"Yeah," he whispered. "But bigger. You're mine, Vina. Mine to protect, mine to go through the ups and downs with, mine to take care of. You don't have to worry about me leaving. Not anymore. You have me. Open your eyes."

Vina squeezed them tight, then opened them and waited to adjust to the dark. They were at the entrance to a property. The fence was old and rusted, and the No Trespassing sign had bullet holes in it.

"I bought this place a few years ago when I was wanting to move out of the clubhouse, but I never really did anything with it. It's just been sitting here." Ramsey got off the motorcycle and pulled a red and black plaid blanket from one of his storage bags and a paper bag of what smelled like sandwiches from the other. He set them beside the bike and helped her off, unclipped her helmet.

"Ramsey," she whispered, realizing what he was doing.

"You had this tradition to Change with your family. And I can see it in you. You're stressed with everything going on, and your eyes change color to your animal's a lot. So I'm making a new tradition for us. This is our place. Just ours. It's our escape from everything. When you need to Change, we'll come here together, and then we'll eat after. And probably fuck because, let's face it, I'm still me and I'm still gonna be a C minus in romance."

"Fucking is good," she said thickly. She didn't care what it said about her, but she found this all very romantic.

Ram gripped her hips and dragged her to him, his smile nothing but pure wickedness. "I *love* when you cuss."

"You've completely corrupted me."

"I know. It's sexy."

She giggled and nuzzled her face against his chest. "Well, I love when you give me sweet surprises. I'm giving you feelings. I'm corrupting you, too."

"Mmm," he rumbled. "Maybe you are. I love when you wear white sneakers." There was a smiling tone to his voice.

"You won't change me so don't even try," she teased, stretching her leg out and pointing the toe of her Chucks.

His eyes went serious, and the smile faded at the corners. "I don't want to change you. You're perfect just how you are."

"I love how you give me butterflies."

Ram wrapped his arms around her shoulders and whispered against her ear, "What else?"

"I love how you listen to me, and when you look at me, you really see me. And how you stick up for me no matter what. I love how you hide the ghosts from your Clan so only you carry the burden. I love that you are a leader, but not power-hungry. You don't just boss people around to make them do stuff. I love how you're honest, fearless, and you care very deeply about your people."

"I love you," he murmured against her ear.

"What?" she gasped.

"You heard me. You fixed me, Vina. I knew exactly where I was headed, and there was no one who could stop my fall. And then you came into that clubhouse, and you caught me. Even when I didn't deserve you, and couldn't pick you back, you caught me. At my worst, you looked at me and said 'no matter what, he's mine.' And now all I see is you. Everything else is secondary, but you…you're everything. You earned my loyalty. I love you."

"Then say it," she whispered. *Please. Say the thing she'd longed to hear. Say the thing she'd dreamed of. Say the thing she'd uttered to him the first time he'd taken her to his bed.*

His lips brushed her earlobe as he murmured with such sincerity, "I'm yours."

And she just…held on. Wrapped her arms so tight around him and held on. She'd been so scared that her fate was to be alone, but everything had changed the moment the matchmaker had set them up. She'd found her mate, and he was better than she could've ever imagined. Tears leaked out of the corners of Vina's eyes as he kissed her worries away.

Tomorrow they would face the public. They would figure out how the Clan would move forward and hunt down the person who bugged the clubhouse. They were right at the edge of a long-brewing storm, and it would be rough waters to navigate for a while. But for tonight, none of that mattered. All that mattered was the man in her arms, swaying them gently from side-to-side, brushing his lips to hers in a silent chant—*I'm yours, I'm yours, I'm yours.*

She'd found her crow, and he wasn't just any crow. He was the King of Crows. Her man, her mate, her future.

This town had never felt like home, and she hadn't been able to understand that until right now.

Home wasn't a place at all. It wasn't a city, or her duplex, or her job, or the clubhouse.

Home was an unbreakable bond her mate had built with her.

It was feeling completely secure in the person she was with.

It was feeling safe to be her exact self, and be loved despite her faults.

It was finding happiness.

It was her mate.

Her. Mate. She'd lucked into something she would never take for granted. Something that she would always covet and protect. Something that she'd waited so long to find.

Home was Ramsey.

Want more of these characters?

For the Hope of a Crow is a standalone series,
but the characters can first bee seen in the
bestselling Outlaw Shifters series.

For more of these characters, check out these other
books from T. S. Joyce.

For the Love of an Outlaw
(Outlaw Shifters, Book 1)

A Very Outlaw Christmas
(Outlaw Shifters, Book 2)

For the Heart of an Outlaw
(Outlaw Shifters, Book 3)

For the Heart of the Warmaker
(Outlaw Shifters, Book 4)

For the Soul of an Outlaw
(Outlaw Shifters, Book 5)

About the Author

T.S. Joyce is devoted to bringing hot shifter romances to readers. Hungry alpha males are her calling card, and the wilder the men, the more she'll make them pour their hearts out. She werebear swears there'll be no swooning heroines in her books. It takes tough-as-nails women to handle her shifters.

She lives in a tiny town, outside of a tiny city, and devotes her life to writing big stories. Foodie, wolf whisperer, ninja, thief of tiny bottles of awesome smelling hotel shampoo, nap connoisseur, movie fanatic, and zombie slayer, and most of this bio is true.

Bear Shifters? Check

Smoldering Alpha Hotness? Double Check

Sexy Scenes? Fasten up your girdles, ladies and gents, it's gonna to be a wild ride.

For more information on T. S. Joyce's work,
visit her website at
www.tsjoyce.com

Made in the USA
Columbia, SC
01 September 2019